PRAISE FOR THE JAMIE JOHNSON SERIES

"You'll read this and want to get out there and play"
Steven Gerrard

"True to the game . . . Dan knows his football"
Owen Hargreaves

"An inspiring read for all football fans"
Gary Lineker

"If you like football, this book's for you"
Frank Lampard

"Jamie could go all the way"
Jermain Defoe

"Pure class – brings the game to life"
Owen Coyle

"I love reading about football and
it doesn't get much better than this"
Joe Hart

"Pure joy"
The Times

"Inspiring"
Observer

"Gripping"
Sunday Express

"A resounding victory"
Telegraph

ABOUT THE AUTHOR

Dan Freedman grew up wanting to be a professional footballer. That didn't happen. But he went on to become a top football journalist, personally interviewing the likes of Cristiano Ronaldo, Lionel Messi, David Beckham and Sir Alex Ferguson. He uses his passion and knowledge of football to write the hugely popular series of Jamie Johnson football novels. When he is not writing, Dan delivers talks and workshops for schools. And he still plays football whenever he can.

www.danfreedman.co.uk
www.jamiejohnson.info
Follow Dan on Twitter @DanFreedman99

DAN FREEDMAN

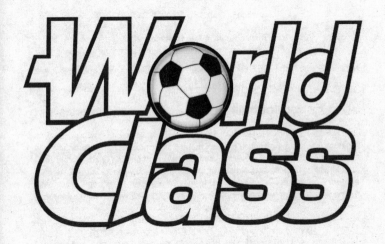

World Class

SCHOLASTIC

First published in the UK in 2011 by Scholastic Children's Books
An imprint of Scholastic Ltd
Euston House, 24 Eversholt Street
London, NW1 1DB, UK
Registered office: Westfield Road, Southam, Warwickshire, CV47 0RA
SCHOLASTIC and associated logos are trademarks and/or registered trademarks of
Scholastic Inc.

This edition published by Scholastic Ltd, 2012

Text copyright © Dan Freedman, 2011
The right of Dan Freedman to be identified as the author of this work
has been asserted by him.

ISBN 978 1407 13479 6

A CIP catalogue record for this book is available from the British Library.

Printed and bound by CPI Group (UK) Ltd, Croydon, CR0 4YY
Papers used by Scholastic Children's Books are made from wood grown in
sustainable forests.

3 5 7 9 10 8 6 4 2

www.scholastic.co.uk/zone

Acknowledgements

Thanks to:

Young Phillip – great idea!

Major for your insights and football feedback.

Caspian Dennis, Ena McNamara, Lola Cashman, Martin Hitchcock, Xabier de Beristain Humphrey and F – for your brilliant advice all along the way.

Ms Pluckrose, Ms Clarke and all the superb secret agents at St Ed's and George Heriot's School for telling me how it is and how it should be!

Jonathan Kaye, Prezzo Restaurants and the Nixon clan for your support.

Hazel Ruscoe – this story is inspired by ideas we had together.

Owen Coyle for getting behind Jamie and the books.

Jason Cox for your imagination and perfect illustrations.

Helen Thomas and the whole team at Scholastic for giving Jamie the freedom to play.

And to you for reading Jamie's story…

Prologue

"We have a saying in football: form is temporary and class is permanent. But world class – genuine world class – well, that's for ever. Are *you* world class? We're about to find out…"

Sir Brian Robertson – Football Manager

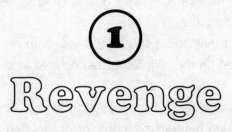

Revenge

The middle of the World Cup

Jamie instantly killed the pace on the ball, deftly cushioning it on his thigh. As it dropped to the ground, he flicked it forwards and sprinted after it in one easy, fluid movement.

Using his perfect close control, he passed the ball from foot to foot, nimbly evading the tackles like a speeding slalom skier racing down a mountain.

With his arms pumping and his legs racing, he galloped down the line. Once he hit turbo speed, Jamie was simply uncatchable.

He was a superhuman playing against mortals. His skills came from another world.

A huge grin was plastered across his face as he teased and destroyed the defenders with his speed and

3

poise. He could beat anyone today and he knew it.

But just at that moment, with Jamie right at the top of his game, displaying the full array of his majestic talent to the watching world, the cruel finger of fate was pointing directly at him.

Disaster was about to call and yet, with his eyes still firmly fixed on the ball, Jamie had no idea at all…

Jamie almost couldn't see through the pain. The torture tore through him like a furious forest fire. Bertorelli had known exactly what he was doing. In an evil scissors motion, he'd wrapped himself around Jamie's knee, crushing it and twisting it, almost until it broke.

Now, as Jamie was lifted on to a stretcher and given oxygen to breathe in, the pain in his brain was almost too much to bear.

All that training … all that practice … all those hours fighting his way back from the last injury. It had all been about this: reaching the World Cup and showing the entire world his skill.

But now Bertorelli had killed those dreams. He'd slashed them apart in cruel, cold-blooded revenge.

Jamie covered his eyes as he was carried away from the pitch into the darkness of the tunnel. He couldn't believe that this was it. That it was all over. It seemed only minutes ago that his World Cup journey had

started with those special letters that came to the
house.

Both of them.

Rewind–
two and a half weeks before the start of the World Cup

(2) Jamie's Choice

Friday 25 May

Jamie picked up the letter and read it again. For the fourth time. No matter how many times he read the words, only two stood out – like flashing lights:

WORLD CUP

THE SCOTTISH FOOTBALL ASSOCIATION

24 May

Dear Jamie Johnson,

It is with great pleasure that I inform you that you have been selected to join Scotland's Provisional World Cup squad. The tournament is being held in England from 11 June – 11 July. Please report, with your passport, to the Scotland Team base: The Riverside Hotel, Buckinghamshire, on 29 May.

Congratulations and good luck.

Sheila Clarke
Team Administrator

Schedule:
29 May – Squad meets
31 May – Warm Up International v Ghana
1 June – Final World Cup Squad Announcement
13 June – First Group D Match v Nigeria
18 June – Second Group D Match v France
23 June – Final Group D Match v Argentina

Dates of further matches will depend on Group Results.

Jamie shook his head and carefully placed the letter on his bed. Then he picked up almost the exact same letter from the England squad.

③

The Ring

Spinning around in circles on the kitchen table, Jamie's ring reflected his mind. Turning this way and that, going around and around but moving nowhere.

Jamie squeezed his head. He felt as if the answer was close to him. Within touching distance. And yet somehow he couldn't reach it.

"I don't see how there's any choice to make," said Jeremy, Jamie's stepdad, barely looking up from his newspaper. "Play for England. They're the hosts, they've actually got a chance of winning the tournament and you'll make more money. Simple. And stop spinning that thing, will you! I'm trying to do the crossword."

"Well, it's not simple to me," said Jamie, purposely ignoring Jeremy and continuing to spin his ring in circles on the kitchen table. Jamie loved that ring. It had been his granddad Mike's and, before that, it had belonged to Mike's dad. It had been passed down from generation to generation and, as Mike had not had a son, he'd left it to Jamie in his will. It was the most precious item Jamie owned.

"What do you reckon Mike would say?" Jamie asked his mum, who was contentedly cradling her cup of tea. "He'd just want me to play for Scotland, wouldn't he?"

Jamie's mum smiled as she sipped her warm cuppa. "Just to see you playing at the World Cup would make Dad the happiest man in the world," she said reassuringly. "He wouldn't care who it was for."

"But what about that?" Jamie said, pointing to the framed photo on the ledge by the kitchen table. It was his mum's favourite: a picture of Jamie as a three-year-old, when his hair was still a bright strawberry-blonde colour. He was smiling and, though he was barely able to run, he was kicking a little football, being proudly supported by his granddad Mike, who was standing just behind him, holding him up.

Jamie liked the photo. He realized that Mike must have been supporting him almost from the day he was born.

"What about it?" asked his mum, turning to look at the photo. "He always said you'd play at a World Cup, you know. I can't believe it's actually coming true!"

"Yeah," said Jamie. "And look at what I'm wearing in the photo."

It was a Scotland shirt.

(4)
Jack

"I can't explain it," mumbled Jamie. "My mind's like ... you know how the bathroom mirror looks after you've had a shower? All misty and that? That's how it feels in my brain. It's all fogged up and I don't know how to get it clear.

"Look at this," he said, handing Jack Marshall his page of scribbled notes. "I've written it all down to try to work it out but I still haven't got a clue what to do."

England or Scotland?!

Decision time!!!! Once I play for one country, I can't change after that so when I decide, that's it. No going back! Urrrgggh too difficult!!!!!

Why England?

Play in the Premiership
Always lived in England
All my coaching and development has been in England
Know most of players, also get to play with Glenn Richardson
Better team = better chance of winning (+ England have got an easy group and Scotland have got the Group of Death!)
England hosting the W Cup - every game will be like a home game
Bigger money and sponsorship (Jeremy!)
Walter Sergeant looks like the oldest football manager in the world. He doesn't inspire me to play for Scotland

Why Scotland?

Mike loved Scotland
He didn't get to play for Scotland but I can do it for him
It's what he would have wanted
Scotland's in my soul

What's best for me?? HELP!!

Jamie looked at his best friend reading his notes. As Jack's big brown eyes scanned the page, he could sense her brilliant brain clicking into action.

She'd always been way cleverer than him. At school she'd got him out of loads of scrapes with her quick thinking and, if necessary, her tae kwon do skills!

And now everyone was going to see exactly how clever she was because one of the biggest TV stations had just hired her to be their pitch-side reporter during the World Cup. Jamie was really pleased for her – and he knew she'd be great – but, at the same time, a little part of him felt as if he wanted to keep her all for himself.

Jack was moving on; making a name for herself in the real world. Sometimes Jamie wondered what that felt like.

"Easy," said Jack, giving Jamie her special smile, as she rested his sheet of notes on her bed.

For a minute Jamie completely zoned out. He was thinking back to all the times he and Jack had spent down at Sunningdale Park, kicking a ball around together. He could still remember the day he beat Jack with a rainbow flick for the first time. He'd trapped the ball behind his ankle and then flicked it up and over his head. It was a wicked, awesome skill but Jack had gone mad at him and made him promise that he'd never do

it again! Jamie had agreed and swore that he wouldn't
– but he'd had his fingers crossed behind his back the
whole time.

"...Why don't you try a trick my dad taught me,"
Jack was suggesting. "Take a coin, say one side is
England and one side is Scotland and then flick it into
the air. Whichever side it lands on, that's your decision
made."

"What?" retorted Jamie, flabbergasted at Jack's
suggestion. "So leave the biggest decision of my career
down to the toss of the coin? Are you serious? That's
a rubbish idea! There's no way I'm going to let a coin
decide for me."

"Ah, but that's the clever bit," grinned Jack, her
perfect white teeth shining back at Jamie. "The coin
isn't there to make the decision for you. It's there
to show you how you feel. If it lands heads and it's
England ... and you feel happy, then it's job done. You
know you wanted to play for England all along. But if
your heart sinks, then you know it's Scotland that you
really want to play for, so you choose them. It's just a
way of showing you how you actually feel."

"Oh, right, I see," said Jamie, taking his scribbled list
back from Jack. "Yeah, that's not bad. Yeah, I quite like
that."

As he looked again at his list, he realized how many

more reasons there were to play for England rather than Scotland. And then his eyes settled on the last item he'd written: "Scotland's in my soul".

If he was honest, Jamie had no idea what that actually meant and yet somehow, at the same time, he had a suspicion that it meant everything.

⑤

Autograph

Sunday 27 May

It was a game of two on two. One of the kids burst through and hammered a shot at the tiny goal.

The ball missed and went flying at the short, stocky teenager who was walking towards them.

"Watch out, mate!" the other players shouted, panicking. The speeding ball was heading straight for the guy's face.

Instinctively, the figure, who was wearing a baseball cap, took two steps back and controlled the ball on his chest. Then he kneed the ball up into the air before volleying it past all four players and into the other mini goal behind them.

The young street footballers, all four of them, stood open-mouthed in wonder. For a second, they were completely noiseless – silenced by the brilliance. They had witnessed something quite extraordinary.

They stared in awe as the mysterious figure walked past them and into the Hawkstone United training ground complex. And that was when they realized.

"Oh my God!" they shouted in astonishment. "It's him! Jamie Johnson! Jamie, wait! Can we have your autograph, please?"

"Sure," said Jamie Johnson, Hawkstone United's star player, taking off his baseball cap to reveal his shortly cropped new haircut and a big, broad smile. Being around kids who liked football always reminded Jamie of how lucky he was. Ten years ago, five years even, he would have been doing exactly what they were doing. Hanging around outside the training ground, kicking a ball around, just on the off chance that they might see a player.

"Can I shake your hand, please?" begged one of the kids. "Oh my days! I'm never washing this hand again – I swear it! My dad says you're the best player he's ever seen!"

"Which school did you go to?" another of the boys shouted. "Was it Kingfield or The Grove? And do you know Robbie Simmonds? He says he's your best mate."

It was like doing the quickest interview of all time!

"I went to both schools," Jamie smiled, while

contending with the flurry of scraps of paper and notepads that were being shoved in front of his face to sign. More and more kids were appearing from nowhere to join the throng. "And yeah, I know Robbie. I went to school with his older brother, Dillon. But don't believe everything he tells you – Robbie's big-time cheeky, he is!"

"So who are you going to play for at the World Cup, then? It's England, isn't it?"

"Not decided yet," said Jamie, waving to the kids as he headed on into the Hawkstone United training complex. "That's what I'm here to talk about."

"Hey, before you go, can you sign my Hawkstone top, please?" asked a boy wearing a shirt with JOHNSON on the back.

"Sure," said Jamie, jogging back.

He took the boy's marker pen and carefully scrawled the new signature that he had been working on.

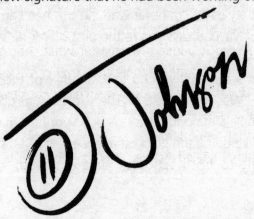

6

That's Life

"You want my advice?" said Archie.

"I need your advice," replied Jamie.

Archie Fairclough's official title at Hawkstone was Assistant Manager, but he was so much more than that to Jamie. Mentor, motivator … doctor even, seeing that he'd been the one to help Jamie back to fitness after his horrific knee injury a couple of years ago. With his barrel chest and his dry sense of humour, Archie had always believed in Jamie – no matter what. And since Mike had died, that meant more than ever.

"Write down a list," suggested Archie. "Put down all the pros and cons—"

"Done that," said Jamie.

"OK, then," smiled Archie. "Here's one for you. You

get a coin, tell yourself that whichever side it lands on—"

"Done that too," Jamie blurted out. "Whichever side it landed on it just felt like I made the wrong choice! Didn't help at all."

"Right," said Archie, subconsciously feeling the white tufts of his beard that Jamie always thought looked like the beginnings of a real Father Christmas look. "I see the problem. You feel a loyalty to both countries."

"Exactly," said Jamie. "I just wish I could play for both!"

"You want to know what I really think, Jamie?" said Archie.

Jamie nodded.

"I don't think it matters which you pick. There are always going to be positives and negatives to every choice. That's life. Get used to it. But I do know one thing for sure: you'd better pick one soon, because time is running out for you – fast."

7
The Call

Jamie had ten minutes before the press conference began. A good time to catch up on missed calls and voicemails. He'd missed a call from a number he hadn't recognized last night.

He dialled in.

"You have … two new messages. First new message received yesterday at 2.26 p.m."

"Jamie! Robbie here! Have you seen my email yet? Come on, mate. I really need this favour. Call me when you can. All right, laters maters!"

Jamie saved the message and shook his head. Robbie

Simmonds was the most confident eleven-year-old in the history of the world. Not many eighteen-year-olds were mates with kids seven years younger than them, but Jamie and Robbie had got on well since the day, a few months ago, that Robbie had challenged Jamie to a game of street football without realizing who Jamie was!

It was clear that Robbie didn't have as much money as other kids his age, and Jamie wondered whether, in the future, he would fall into the trap of stealing the things that he wanted because he couldn't afford to buy them. That would be sad because Robbie had so much going for him; he was a funny, cheeky kid and a brilliantly skilful young footballer too. Sometimes Robbie reminded Jamie of himself. Having said that, Jamie would never have used a phrase like "laters maters" – it didn't even make sense!

"Second new message received yesterday at 10.41 p.m."

"Jamie, this is Brian Robertson here. Listen, I'm going to be managing Scotland at the World Cup. Walter Sergeant's just been admitted to hospital with a stroke. He's going to be OK but there's no way he can take a team to the World Cup. The news will come out tomorrow. Anyway, I'm going to do it and you're the

first call I'm making. I want to ask you not to make a decision on England or Scotland until we've spoken.

I want you to play for us, Jamie. I've looked at the squad and the steel is there. Those players are solid as a rock. It just needs a bit of creativity to go with it. A bit of silk. It needs you, Jamie. You're the final piece in the jigsaw, the key to our success. I just know it.

I lost you at Foxborough, Jamie. There's no way I'm going to let you slip through my fingers again. Anyway, don't do anything until we've spoken and call me back when you get this message. It's urgent."

"End of new messages. To hear saved messages press—"

Jamie's fumbling fingers put his phone back into his pocket as he stood for a second in complete and utter shock. There was no doubt about it – that was definitely the real Sir Brian Robertson. Jamie would recognize that voice anywhere. With eleven Premier League titles for Foxborough under his belt, Robertson was the most successful manager in the history of British football – a living legend. This changed everything. With him in charge, Scotland would suddenly be a completely different proposition: a team to be reckoned with.

Injury had prevented Jamie from working with Robertson when he was on Foxborough's books as a youngster, and that was something he'd always regretted. But now, out of the blue, here was another chance to realize his dream of playing under his favourite manager. It would be fantasy football, Jamie Johnson style.

There was only one problem.

It was too late.

Jamie had already chosen England.

Making
Headlines

Wednesday 30 May

Johnson Picks England

After being selected by both England and Scotland, prodigy Premier League star Jamie Johnson last night nailed his international colours to England's mast, telling a press conference: "I couldn't turn down the Three Lions."

There has been a considerable amount of speculation since it first became B...

Robertson loses Johnson again

Having released Jamie Johnson from Foxborough as a youngster – subsequently calling it "the biggest mistake of my career" – new Scotland boss Sir Brian Robertson lost Johnson for the second time last night despite a last-ditch phone call to get the winger to change his mind.

elephant!

Winger to make Three Lions Debut

EIGHTEEN-year-old Johnson, who will win his first England cap in tomorrow's friendly international against Greece, said that the last few days had been "agonizing" but that he was happy with his final choice. Bookmakers, meanwhile, have reported a sudden flurry of bets on England to win the World Cup as a result of Johnson's decision.

* * *

9
Five Star

The England team hotel

From: Robbie
To: Jamie [JJ@JamieJohnson.info]
Date: 29 May 12.24 p.m.
Subject:

All right Jamie Boy! Guess what? I'm gonna let u do me a favour! I want 2B a ballboy at the World Cup! Then I can show evry1 my skills just like u did when u were a mascot 4 Hawkstone! Go on, Jamie Boy! I know u can do it! U gotta do it for UR best mate Robbie! I'll even be nice to you when UR retired and I'm the big star!

Cool, tell me when it's done.

Peace and love, man!

Rob the God!

PS – Dillon says hi and says he swears he was a better player than you at school. He says even you'll admit it. But, don't worry, I told him to go and stick his stupid head down the toilet!

Jamie couldn't help laughing even though he was also trying to listen to Michelle, the England Team Administrator, who was explaining all the details about the journey to the stadium for the game against Greece that night.

"So kick off is at eight o'clock," she was saying. "And the coach leaves here at six-fifteen."

"Isn't that a bit late?" asked Jamie, alarmed at the prospect of missing his England debut because of the traffic around Wembley. If there was one thing that Jeremy had drummed into Jamie since he'd become his stepdad, it was the importance of never being late for anything.

"It's OK," smiled Michelle. "We've done this a few times so you can leave the arrangements to us. We get a police escort all the way from the hotel. It shouldn't take more than twenty minutes."

"Oh, right," laughed Jamie, realizing his error. "Yeah … I knew that! I always get a police escort wherever I go! Oh – one thing I do need to ask you. Can I have your email address, please?"

"What?" she asked. "Why?" She seemed a little flustered and her face was beginning to turn red.

"It's OK," Jamie grinned. "I'm not gonna stalk you or anything! I just need you to help me sort out a favour – for a friend."

⑩ Get Out of Jail

Jamie could not believe the size of his room. It was massive! Pretty much the same size as the house he and his mum had moved into after his dad had left when Jamie was very young. He had two double beds and he was the only one staying in the room.

Jamie had stayed in some posh hotels with Hawkstone, but this pad, with its own golf course and two swimming pools, was something else. It was the kind of place you could imagine kings staying in. The servants – Jamie didn't know what else to call them – had put rose petals on his bed the night before and even pulled the sheets down so the duvet was easier to get under.

Jamie was just about to text Jack a picture of his

bath, which was deep enough to dive into, when the breaking news banner popped up on the TV.

It was the news that Jamie had been dreading for months. The news that threatened him in so many ways. Transfixed to the screen, he sat down to watch.

BREAKING NEWS: Mattheus Bertorelli released from prison ... Hawkstone forward wins appeal against match-fixing conviction...

The reports showed Bertorelli, standing outside the court, reading from a prepared statement. He spoke in Spanish, with an English translator by his side: "This is a great day for me and my family. We have been through a terrible ordeal that was completely unnecessary. I want to thank everyone at home in Argentina for their support. I'm going to undergo an intense fitness regime to be ready for the World Cup and I promise I will bring back the trophy for you. It is my destiny. It is our destiny. Justice will come to those who are responsible."

As Bertorelli and his family started to walk away, a journalist shouted out in English: "And what message do you have for the people that accused you of match fixing, Mattheus? Would you ever lose a game on purpose for money?"

Jamie shifted uncomfortably in his seat. He felt a cold, glistening sweat start to creep down his forehead. He was the one who had accused Bertorelli of match fixing, but he did not feel guilty about what he'd done. No way. Bertorelli had accepted bribes to throw Hawkstone games and that made him the worst kind of cheat. When Jamie had found out, he'd had no choice but to tell people and make sure Bertorelli got the punishment he deserved. But now, with Bertorelli out of prison, suddenly everything was different. It was Jamie who felt under attack.

He stared at Bertorelli's face through the television. Gone was the long black hair and perma-tanned skin which had won Bertorelli scores of modelling and endorsement contracts. Now, after nearly two months in prison, his head was shaved and his face had become thinner and paler. But above all it was his eyes that stood out. They were burning with anger and Jamie knew full well who that fury and resentment was reserved for.

"In Argentina, we have a saying," he said. His accent was as thick as ever and his voice rough and gravelly. "If you fight a bull, you must kill him, because if you don't, the bull will take revenge."

"What do you mean?" asked the reporter. "Are you saying you want revenge?"

Jamie turned off the TV. He couldn't listen to any more of this.

He looked at his hands. They were shaking.

Bertorelli could not have made his threat any clearer.

Take Away

England v Greece
friendly international at Wembley
KICK-OFF 8 p.m.

Jamie settled into his seat on the England Team coach. It was, without doubt, the classiest coach he had ever been on. The soft, smooth leather interior oozed luxury as Jamie slid into it.

Every seat had a built-in TV screen but none of the channels were showing the Scotland game, so he turned it off and tuned into the radio commentary on his phone instead…

"…And if you're just joining us here at Hampden Park,

the news is that, with half an hour gone, Scotland are currently drawing nil-nil in this friendly international with Ghana..."

Hampden Park. Just hearing that name brought all the memories back for Jamie. Going over to Mike's to watch international football. They recorded the England games and always watched them later, but Mike insisted that Scotland came first. He was mad about Scotland and had to watch all their games live. He would sing all the words to the national anthem at the top of his voice and, if Scotland went on to win the game, he would be bursting with pride.

The deal was always the same. If Scotland were winning at half-time, they would order a Chinese takeaway. If not, it was cheese on toast.

Jamie didn't know whether Mike had intended it that way, but the incentive of the takeaway ended up meaning that Jamie always celebrated Scotland goals just as much as Mike!

"And here now, the big Scotland striker, Duncan Farrell, seizes possession of the ball on the edge of the area. What's he going to do? Is he going to take on the strike? Oh he issssssssssssss! What a goal!!!!! What an absolute belter!! Farrell struck that so hard it almost

broke the back of the net!!"

Even though he tried his best to push his excitement back down, it was no use; Jamie just couldn't keep quiet.

"Youuu beauty!" he roared, launching himself out of his seat and punching the air.

Suddenly, as he looked around, he became aware that every single England player and member of the coaching staff was staring at Jamie as though he were a complete madman.

Jamie quickly sat back down and, trying to pretend that nothing had happened, tilted his head to look innocently out of the window.

The unmistakeable shape of the Wembley Arch was now coming clearly into view ahead of them.

Jamie licked his lips and smiled. He was sure he could taste Chinese.

The International

**Friendly international at
Wembley Stadium – 61 minutes played**

England 3 - 0 Greece
G Richardson, 20
V Bickham, 41
C Dennis, 58

Jamie saw the substitution board go up and left his seat on the England bench.

A wave of excitement rippled through the crowd. With England comfortably winning 3-0 and the game over as a contest, this was the moment that so many of them had been waiting for – Jamie Johnson's England debut.

Jamie walked over to the touchline. He could feel

his heart begin to flutter with a mixture of anticipation and nerves. He was about to reach the highest level of football.

He was about to become an international footballer.

"And a substitution for England!" said the stadium announcer while the Fourth Official checked Jamie's studs. Jamie looked on to the pitch and started to visualize the moves he wanted to make tonight. He wanted to give this crowd something to cheer about. He was going to entertain them. He was ready—

"You will need to take off the ring now," said the Fourth Official in a strong, German-sounding accent, pointing to Jamie's finger.

"This?" said Jamie. "Can't I just cover it up?"

"No. It is still dangerous for the other players. So please, you must take off the ring now."

Jamie didn't like this. He had worn the ring every day since Mike had died. But it seemed he had no choice. If he wanted to make his international debut, he had to remove it. Slowly, reluctantly, he slid the ring from his finger. The skin underneath seemed pale and white – unnatural somehow. Jamie was about to hand the ring over but before he did so, he took one last look. And that was when he saw them.

The four words that had been inscribed on the inside of the ring:

Keep The Tartan Pride

The words, engraved in the gold, seemed to shine out like a lighthouse in the dark.

Keep The Tartan Pride

The answer *had* been there all along. It was just that Jamie hadn't been able to see it.

"You must give it to me now," said the Fourth Official, tugging the ring from Jamie's fingers.

"Coming off, number 7, Glenn Richardson, and coming on, to make his England debut, number 15, Jamie Johnson!"

"I don't have to do anything," said Jamie, grabbing the ring away and putting it back on his finger. Back where it belonged.

"But I will not be letting you on the pitch with it on," said the now-panicking Fourth Official. "That is the rule."

"That's no problem," said Jamie, stepping backwards, away from the pitch, as a murmur of confusion now spread like a Mexican wave around Wembley. "Because

I'm not coming on anyway."

"But the substitution is being made now. It is too late to change your mind!"

Not quite, Jamie said to himself. *Not quite*.

And with that, he turned around and – first in a jog, then in a sprint – headed back down the tunnel.

At last Jamie had listened to his heart and it had told him exactly what to do.

For the first time in weeks, Jamie knew just where he was going.

⑬
Good Knight

Friday 1 June – 11.58 p.m.

"Welcome, Jamie," said Sir Brian Robertson, stretching out his hand as he stood by the entrance of the Scotland Team hotel.

It was late at night but Jamie had got a cab down to Buckinghamshire as soon as it had been confirmed that Scotland had beaten the deadline and been allowed to include Jamie in their final World Cup squad. After Jamie had called Sir Brian from Wembley last night, there had been a frantic rush to get all the paperwork done in time. Thankfully they had beaten the midnight deadline by minutes.

Jamie looked at Sir Brian Robertson. He might have been in his sixties but he was still a fit and strong-looking man. The two had not spoken properly since the day Jamie had his accident as a young player at Foxborough. That was a long time ago and Jamie had grown up since then, but there was still something about Robertson which made Jamie feel like a little boy again.

Robertson's reputation went before him. Everyone in football knew that you didn't argue with Sir Brian Robertson – you just listened.

"Thanks, boss," said Jamie. "I'm glad to be here."

"So am I," smiled Robertson, putting his arm around Jamie. "So am I."

Jamie unpacked and had a look around his new room. Only one double bed this time and just a normal sized bath – Jamie was almost disappointed! He could see how some players quickly got spoilt. He'd only spent a couple of days in the England hotel but he had already started getting used to the VIP treatment. Still, it wasn't as if he was slumming it with Scotland now; the Riverside Hotel had five stars by its name, it had beautiful gardens backing on to the Thames and it even had its own hairdresser's! Not that Jamie would be requiring a visit – he used clippers these days to keep his hair really short.

Jamie fished the World Cup Guide from the evening paper out of his bag. He'd been reading it in the cab on the way down but he'd saved the Scotland section to read before bed. He was late in joining up with the squad so this would be a good way to get to learn everything about the players who were about to become his new teammates.

World Cup

Your Ultimate Guide To Keep

Our Special Profiles on Scotland's Key Men

THE BOSS

Sir Brian Robertson
Position: Manager
Age: 61
Games as Scotland Manager: 1
Wins: 1

Walter Sergeant's illness may have been untimely but, in convincing Sir Brian Robertson to step in and take up the reins for the tournament, Scotland have pulled off a masterstroke. The managerial legend has won everything there is to win at club level and will fancy pitting his wits against the world's best.

Strength: Finest motivator in the game. Powers of communication and psychology are such that one former player famously said: "Sir Brian could convince a donkey to win the Grand National!"

Weakness: This is his first crack at international management. His swashbuckling style of football may work in the Premier League, but how will it fare at the World Cup?

LAST LINE OF DEFENCE

Allie Stone
Position: Keeper
Squad Number: 1
Age: 27
Caps: 39

Strength: Charismatic figure in the dressing room and capable of outstanding reflex saves.

Weakness: Clearly carrying a few extra pounds. Won't be winning any 50/50 races to the ball.

THE SKIPPER

Cameron McManus (Captain)
Position: Centre Half
Squad Number: 5
Age: 28
Caps: 37
Goals: 5

Strength: Leadership and bravery. Former builder before turning pro, whose no-nonsense approach personified Scotland's heroic march to qualification. Not a big talker – on or off the pitch – but hugely respected by his teammates. Leads by example.

Weakness: Pace. Might struggle to contend with nippy, fast attackers.

Jamie's eyes scanned ahead to the attackers. He hoped they had him down as one of the "Key Men" but the only attacker they featured was:

BATTERING RAM

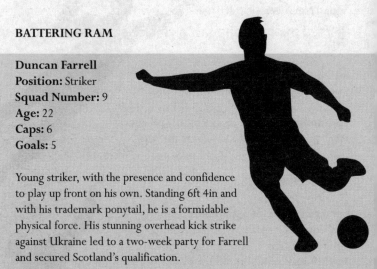

Duncan Farrell
Position: Striker
Squad Number: 9
Age: 22
Caps: 6
Goals: 5

Young striker, with the presence and confidence to play up front on his own. Standing 6ft 4in and with his trademark ponytail, he is a formidable physical force. His stunning overhead kick strike against Ukraine led to a two-week party for Farrell and secured Scotland's qualification.

Strength: Heading. An unparalleled leap makes him virtually unbeatable in the air. Also has a shot like a sledgehammer.

Weakness: Discipline. Notoriously bad at taking orders. Said he would never play for Scotland again after former manager Walter Sergeant tried to substitute him against Croatia. Farrell refused to leave the pitch. A maverick talent who does not take well to authority. It will be interesting to see how Robertson handles him.

Jamie went back and scanned all the profiles again. Not even a mention of him! Maybe the paper had gone to print before Jamie had announced that he was going to play for Scotland. Or maybe they just didn't rate him as one of Scotland's key players. Either way he was still disappointed not to have his own profile. But then he turned the page and saw a whole spread dedicated just to him!

STAR MAN

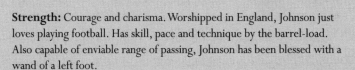

Jamie Johnson *
Position: Winger
Squad Number: 11
Age: 18
Caps: 0

The fearless winger may be small but he uses his low centre of balance and electric pace to dance away from defenders with ease. Has everything in his locker to be one of the brightest stars of the World Cup. Indeed, this tournament could be his passport to an even bigger stage, as he is reported to have already caught the eye of several of Europe's superclubs.

Strength: Courage and charisma. Worshipped in England, Johnson just loves playing football. Has skill, pace and technique by the barrel-load. Also capable of enviable range of passing, Johnson has been blessed with a wand of a left foot.

Weakness: His temper may be an issue. Has already been sent off three times in his career. Finds it difficult to control his anger. Opponents will look to exploit this. Is he simply too young?

*Subject to Scotland beating Fifa deadline to register the player.

5 THINGS YOU DIDN'T KNOW
ABOUT SCOTLAND'S STAR MAN

- James Michael Johnson was born in Hawkstone and has just turned 18 (birthday 18 May).

- First came to prominence when, as mascot for Hawkstone United aged 11, he scored an overhead kick!

- Was so good at school his teacher stopped him using his wand of a left foot in practice matches.

- Puts his football skills down to his grandfather – a Scottish youth international whose career was cut short by a knee injury at 17.

- His favourite foods are Chinese and chicken and chips but limits himself to eating them only once a month!

Jamie closed the pull-out. Although he was glad that they had named him as the Star Man, he still felt a bit annoyed. Not because they had pointed out that he had problems controlling his temper – Jamie accepted that. It was true; sometimes he lost it. That was just the way he was.

And it didn't bother him that they had questioned his age either; in football, if you were good enough, you were old enough. Everyone knew that.

No, it was actually the bit where they had written

earlier in the piece that he'd been "blessed" to have such a good left foot that had got up Jamie's nose.

Yes, it was true that he'd been lucky to have been born with some natural talent – so were thousands of people. But that was only half of the deal. Everything else was down to pure hard work. And a story Mike had once told him. Well, told him lots of times, in fact.

Every Christmas without fail, Mike had told Jamie the exact same story about the day one bad pass had almost killed him. It had happened when Mike was a ten-year-old kid growing up in Scotland. He'd been playing football with his brothers one afternoon and he'd made a really bad pass, kicking the ball into a river by mistake. His brothers – both older than him – had forced him to go in and get the ball back but, because the river had been almost frozen, Mike had ended up contracting pneumonia. It had been such a severe case that he'd ended up in hospital and had almost died! And all because of one bad pass.

So, from the moment that Jamie had started playing football, Mike had constantly drummed into him that the aim of the game was not to kick the ball. It was to keep it. He'd made Jamie promise that he would practise his passing every single day of his life and Jamie had not let him down.

Even now, he still stayed on for hours after training, honing his skills to become the best player that he could possibly be.

That was why Jamie didn't like it when people said that he had been "blessed". He wasn't lucky. Someone hadn't just "given him" the ability that he had today. He'd earned it.

And tomorrow, in his first World Cup training session with Scotland, he'd need to prove that once again to his new teammates, all of whom would be waiting to see exactly what Jamie Johnson could do.

There was just one last thing left to do before getting into bed. Jamie opened up the World Cup Guide and ripped the Wall Chart out of the centre pages.

It had all the groups, all the teams and the match schedule for the entire tournament. Jamie would fill it in after every game. As he stuck the chart to the wall in his room, Jamie's eyes were drawn like magnets to the two spaces left for the teams that would contest the World Cup Final on 11 July at Wembley.

The World Cup Final. The biggest game on earth. What Jamie would give to play in a game like that...

14

Bottom Line

Saturday 2 June – breakfast

Jamie wanted to get a good feed in before his first training session with his new teammates. The problem was, he didn't know what to choose. There were scrambled eggs, poached eggs, mushrooms, tomatoes and lots of—

"Baked beans! My favourite!" said Allie Stone, Scotland's huge goalkeeper, who was lining up behind Jamie in the queue for breakfast. He'd just become the first member of the squad to speak to Jamie.

"Beans give me rocket fuel, if you know what I mean!" he smiled. "Allie Stone – nice to meet you."

And without a hint of warning, Allie let rip with what sounded like a ginormous, improbably loud fart. It sounded more like a trumpet noise than anything a human body should naturally be able to create.

At first Jamie wasn't entirely sure that he'd heard right. Would a footballer really stand there, in the middle of a World Cup training camp, farting his head off? But, then, almost immediately, Jamie heard it again. And this time it was entirely unmistakeable. As was the huge grin plastered across Allie Stone's face.

The fact that not a soul had even turned to acknowledge the loudness of Allie's backfiring was a sure indication that this was far from unusual behaviour for the big man. This fellow was, quite clearly, a formidable farter.

"All right, Allie, nice to meet you," said Jamie, trying to ignore the continual noises being produced by his new goalkeeper's rear end.

"Call me Stonefish," said the big keeper, offering one of his humongous hands for Jamie to shake. He had a friendly smile – revealing the absence of four front teeth – and exuded an uncomplicated kind of warmth which immediately made Jamie feel comfortable in his presence.

"OK, will do, Stonefish!" said Jamie, carefully loading a poached egg on to his toast, trying not to tear the thin layer of egg white that housed the yolk.

"Yeah, we all have nicknames here," announced Stonefish.

"Oh, right – so how come yours is Stonefish?" asked Jamie, struggling to hold in his laughter as Allie Stone produced another real whopper. Was there no end to this man's wind?

"God knows!" laughed Stonefish as he piled a fourth spoonful of baked beans on to his plate. "Treach is the man who gives out the names."

Jamie knew who Stonefish was talking about. Ronnie Treacher was the other left winger in the squad and Jamie had heard that he wasn't too happy about Jamie joining up with Scotland at such a late stage.

Feeling a little like the kid who wants to make new friends on the first day at school, Jamie poured himself some orange juice and looked around the hotel breakfast room for somewhere to sit.

In the corner was the big ponytailed striker, Duncan Farrell. He was alone and looked as if he didn't want to be disturbed. Meanwhile, on another table, the captain, Cameron McManus, and his centre-half partner, Owen Tulley, were deep in conversation, so Jamie was happy to see Stonefish waving him over to join him.

Stonefish lifted his leg from his seat and let out a little high-pitched squeaker by way of welcoming Jamie to the table.

Then, just as Jamie was sitting down, Stonefish slapped him on the back and said, "Ah – speak of the devil. Here comes Treach."

Jamie watched Ronnie Treacher take a seat opposite them. He was a thin, wiry man with curly black hair that was greying at his temples.

"So what nickname are we gonna give to Jamie then?" Stonefish asked Treacher cheerily. "Poor little soul feels left out without a nickname of his own."

"At Hawkstone they call me SatNav," Jamie added eagerly.

But Ronnie Treacher turned and gave Jamie the kind of withering look a wrestler might give an opponent before clotheslining him. Jamie gulped and felt the smile drop off his face.

Treacher had piercing weasel-like eyes perched closely together above a broken nose, and they were homed in directly on Jamie.

"Why is that then?" he said finally, in a voice that could not have sounded more bitter if he'd tried.

"Because my passes and crosses always find their destination," said Jamie proudly.

"Yeah?" replied Treacher. "I thought it was because you've got an annoying voice and you keep talking when everyone wishes you'd just shut up."

For a second, Jamie laughed, thinking it was a joke. Then he realized Treacher wasn't smiling. The message was simple. Not every member of the Scotland squad was entirely happy to have Jamie on board.

"Put your money where your mouth is," challenged Allie Stone, bouncing up and down on his goal line. "Fifty quid says you can't score a penalty against me!"

The two of them were the last ones out on to the training pitch. The session had gone well and Jamie had lashed in five goals in the practice match. But he still wanted to work some more on his finishing, so he'd asked Stonefish to stay on to help him out. That was when the bet had come up.

"You're on," said Jamie, quickly putting the ball down before Stonefish changed his mind. He hadn't missed a penalty in about five years. This was going to be easy money.

Then, as Jamie took three steps back, Allie Stone started a routine the likes of which Jamie had never seen before. It was obviously designed to put Jamie off.

First Stonefish started headbutting the post; then he jumped on to the ground and began break-dancing horrifically in the grass, before finally jumping up to hang from the crossbar, making screeching chimpanzee-like sounds as he swung in the air.

Jamie shook his head and concentrated on what he had to do. The World Cup was just around the corner. He was going to have to put up with worse than this during the tournament and besides, he'd already decided what he was going to do with this spot kick. Top corner. Right-hand side.

Jamie sprinted up to the ball and was just about to strike it home when he looked up to see that Allie Stone had pulled down his shorts and his pants and was now doing a full-scale moony right in Jamie's face.

Jamie couldn't believe what he was seeing. He ended up smacking the ball right into Stonefish's bare bottom. It was as though his backside was a magnet to the ball!

The ball belted straight into Stonefish's behind before ballooning high over the bar, and although the powerful impact had left a big, round, red impression the size of a football on his bottom, the keeper turned around with a look of pure jubilation etched across his face.

"Fifty quid!" he shouted triumphantly, dancing around his goal, smacking his big bum as he went. "You owe me fifty quid. That's the bottom line, my friend – now show me the money!!"

⑮ Called Up

Tuesday 12 June – the day before Scotland's first World Cup Group game v Nigeria

"Seriously, Brian. How far do you think you can take this team – *realistically*? This is Scotland, remember?"

The manager had to do an official press conference before every game. It was a difficult proposition, not least because the journalists all worked in a pack, latching on to any misplaced word, attempting to take advantage and get a headline.

But it was always worth watching a Brian Robertson press conference. He took the journalists on at their own game. It was a war he enjoyed waging.

"Who knows how far we can go?" he said. "But I'll tell you something right now – me and my squad have not just come here to make up the numbers. Obviously

I'm looking forward to seeing Germany and Brazil both play their first games tonight, but from what I've seen of the tournament so far, I don't think there's anything for us to fear, so there's no reason why we can't go all the way."

The journalists could not help but let their amusement show.

"But you can't expect us to believe that you can suddenly turn this lot into World Cup winners. Come on, Sir Brian, you're in the Group of Death – even qualifying for the next round's a pretty long shot, isn't it?"

"To be frank with you, I couldn't care less what you think," Robertson responded. "It's what my players believe, that's what counts. You lot can sit there and giggle as much as you want – I can see you. But don't expect me to hang around to watch it. I've got a World Cup to win."

And with that, Sir Brian Robertson stood up and strode out of the room.

Watching in his hotel room, Jamie stared wide-eyed at his TV. That was the way this tournament was going to be, he'd realized; this bunch of players and the manager against the world.

And he very much sensed that this was just how Sir Brian Robertson liked it.

Jamie strode towards it. It was over thirty centimetres tall, made entirely of gold and, to Jamie, it was the most beautiful thing in the world.

His hat-trick had blown away the opposition and now it was time for him to collect his prize.

Just like Bobby Moore at Wembley all those years ago, Jamie wiped his hands clean on his jersey and took the glorious prize firmly in his hands. Then he kissed the World Cup trophy and lifted it high into the—

Suddenly Jamie was awake. The aggressive siren of the hotel phone by his bed was boxing his ears.

Jamie opened his heavy eyes and stretched over to the side of the bed.

"Hello?" he said wearily, still trying to track down his senses.

At first there was no sound on the other end of the line, but then slowly it started: the breathing. Heavy, aggressive breathing. It sent a shudder down Jamie's back as if a spider had crawled down his spine.

"Who is this?" demanded Jamie, anger and fear replacing his sleepiness.

Still the breathing. If anything now more threatening.

"I know it's you, Bertorelli!" growled Jamie, sitting bolt upright in his bed. "When are you going to get it into your thick head that I didn't do anything wrong? I just told the police what you were up to. You're a cheat and a criminal and you got what you deserved!"

Heavy, ominous breathing.

Jamie thought back to what Bertorelli had said on the TV – that he wanted revenge.

"I'm not scared of you either," barked Jamie, but the tremor of fear in his voice said otherwise. "And I'm having this phone monitored, so you best not be calling me again!"

And with that Jamie slammed down the phone before unplugging it at the socket.

He tried to get back to sleep, but it was no use. His adrenaline was pumping and his eyes were wide open, staring into the darkness that surrounded him.

It wasn't just this phone call that had disturbed Jamie, or the timing of it – the night before Scotland's first group match – it was the fact that this had now happened for four nights in a row.

Tomorrow the whole world would be watching him play football. But tonight, as a clock somewhere in the hotel struck 1 a.m., Jamie felt vulnerable and completely on his own.

Magic Word

Wednesday 13 June

Jamie was one of the first on the team bus and took one of the prized seats on the back row. He wanted to get settled, get his match head on and focus on the specific instructions Brian Robertson had given him in the pre-match meeting: if he didn't get any joy going down the line in the first twenty minutes, Jamie had been instructed to switch wings so that he could cut inside from the right flank and power in some thunderbolt shots at the goal.

Jamie was just trying to visualize himself firing a cataclysmic masterblaster into the roof of the net when a group of his teammates clambered over him to look out of the window back at the hotel.

"Look at her! She's fit as!" the lads were saying,

pointing at a girl who was waving the team coach off as it departed.

"Hey, look. She's waving at me!"

"No, you egg! She's waving at me!"

Jamie looked at the girl. He knew who she was. She worked in the hair salon in the hotel and she'd smiled at him the other day when he'd walked past.

Jamie knew why the other lads were taken with her – she had shiny blonde hair and bright blue eyes – but he wasn't interested. He already had his eyes on someone else.

"Oi, PratNav – you're in my seat," said a menacing voice, rudely interrupting Jamie's pre-match focus.

Jamie looked up to see Ronnie Treacher. He did not seem happy.

"I said: you're in my seat," he snarled, his thin, gaunt features tightening with anger.

"Oh, right," said Jamie, preparing to get up and move somewhere else. If he was honest, he could understand that Treacher was upset. Jamie had taken his place in the team and no footballer ever liked the feeling of being dropped – especially not for a World Cup game.

"Move!"

Now *that* Jamie didn't like. There were ways of doing things and he didn't like the way Treacher was doing this. If he'd asked Jamie politely to swap seats, there wouldn't have been a problem. But speaking to Jamie like this – as though he were a piece of dirt – was just guaranteed to wind Jamie up. Generally, Jamie didn't go looking for trouble but if it came to him, he had no problem standing up for himself.

"Sorry, mate," said Jamie, holding his ground. "Does it have your name on it?"

"I've been sitting in this seat on *our* coach for the last twelve years, you fool," barked Treacher. Jamie noticed that his ashen face seemed to have been stained a permanent yellowy-grey colour by the cigarettes everyone knew he secretly smoked each night. "I was playing for Scotland when you were still in nappies. Show some respect!"

"Yeah, well, respect works both ways, Ronnie," replied Jamie. "Instead of just telling me to move, why don't you try using the magic word for a change?"

Treacher's lip started to bend and twitch with fury.

"Magic word?" he snarled. "Fine: I want you to move … NOW!"

"Here, Tommy," said Jamie, handing his gold ring to the Scotland kit man, Tommy McAvennie, as they arrived in the dressing room. "They won't let me play with it on, so can you look after this for me during the match, please? But be careful with it – it's the most valuable thing I own."

Tommy was a big man with a broad smile. He'd had a bit of a shady past and it was well known that he was a heavy gambler but, for some reason that he couldn't quite explain, Jamie felt as though he could trust the man with anything even though they'd only just met.

"No probs," smiled Tommy. "It's safe with me."

"Thanks," said Jamie, before proudly adding: "Take a look at the inscription if you want."

"Keep the Tartan Pride," read Tommy, before putting the ring in his pocket and giving Jamie a reassuring grin. "Aye – too right. Who gave you that?"

"It was my granddad's," explained Jamie. "I called him Mike though, because we were mates. He was my top man… Anyway…" said Jamie, catching himself before he slipped into sadness. "I'll get it back off you after the game."

Jamie surveyed the fruit basket in the dressing room and picked up a banana. But, as soon as he started to peel it, he had to put it straight back down. Realizing that there were only forty minutes to go until kick-off, Jamie suddenly started to feel more than a little queasy.

So much had happened in the last few days that, in a way, the actual match had kind of crept up on him.

And now it was here. Everything that he had grown

up watching: the flags, the painted faces, the packed stadium… He was about to become a part of it… His football dream was about to come true…

Jamie was about to play at the World Cup finals.

⑰
Toilet Humour

20 minutes to kick-off

With his stomach rapidly feeling more and more as though it was on some kind of roller-coaster ride, Jamie headed to the toilets to try to take care of business. The last thing he wanted was to be caught short on the pitch!

Ronnie Treacher was already standing at the urinals when Jamie walked in. Seeing Jamie, Treacher turned and headed straight out of the toilets, completely blanking him.

"Where I was brought up we were taught to wash our hands after we've been to the toilet," said Jamie, unable to resist a little dig at the man who'd been so rude to him earlier. He was actually pretty happy to have come up with that line off the cuff, despite his nausea.

1-0 to Jamie Johnson!

"Yeah, well, where I come from we learnt not to aim at our hands in the first place," replied Treacher, shoulder-barging his way past Jamie as he left.

1-1.

Now he was alone, Jamie looked at himself in the mirror. His face was a greyish-green colour and he could feel his mouth beginning to fill with sweet-tasting saliva – a familiar warning sign that Jamie's body was preparing itself to be sick.

It felt like a dark poison. Swelling first in his stomach, then rising quickly up into his chest and throat. There was no way Jamie was going to be able to stop it.

He ran into the cubicle and just managed to lift up the lid before the entire contents of his belly projected out of his mouth in a stinking stream of vomit.

He was sick with extreme violence; half-digested bits of carrot, sweetcorn and orange all spurted so powerfully into the water that they splashed back up and into Jamie's face.

Jamie caught his breath and, for a second, tried to calm his tremoring body before another, unexpected wave of vomit rushed from his mouth. He kept retching even when his stomach had nothing left to give.

Finally, after hanging his limp head over the bowl for a couple more minutes, the heaving of his stomach began to subside, allowing his senses to return.

He wiped his mouth clean with toilet paper and then went to the sink to splash ice-cold water on his face. He even slapped his cheeks to get the blood racing again.

Jamie had never believed the stories he'd heard about other players being sick before matches due to nerves. He'd thought it was all made up.

"How can someone be nervous about playing football?" he'd always joked. "It's supposed to be fun!"

But now Jamie understood why. This was the World Cup. The whole world was watching. And after all, he was the "Star Man" – everyone would be expecting him to deliver.

⑱
Sing to Win

Jamie tapped the sign above his head as he'd seen so many footballers do on TV.

THIS IS
ANFIELD

Great players, awesome players, world class players had played upon this turf and now Jamie was following in their footsteps.

It all happened in a blur. Walking out on to the pitch, the explosion of noise and colour, the deafening roar from the Tartan Army, the national anthems and realizing he didn't know all the words, the handshakes, the team photo, the referee putting the whistle to his lips…

Jamie looked around, trying to take in the atmosphere for the last time before the game started.

That was when he saw her.

Standing by the tunnel with her notebook in her hand.

Her hair was tied up and she had make-up on.

For a second, Jamie forgot where he was. All he could see was Jack. He thought back to when his best friends at school had told him that Jack was untouchable, out of his league.

But Jamie had never believed them. He knew Jack better than they wished they could.

He looked at her, smiled and sent her a wave.

It was at that moment that Jamie's heart sank. She might have been a long way away, over on the other side of the pitch. And she might have been concentrating on her work, but Jamie had still expected Jack to wave back.

GROUP D
Scotland v Nigeria
Anfield
KICK-OFF 3 p.m.

After the initial roar that accompanied the kick-off, Anfield fell silent. It was waiting… It was expectant.

And it was to remain that way. Nigeria's tactics –

they were playing three men in the middle of midfield, two of them holding – were suffocating Scotland in the centre of the park, preventing them getting the ball out to the wings. Meanwhile, Nigeria always looked dangerous with their incredible pace on the break.

At times, Jamie would go minutes without even getting a touch. He tried switching wings as Robertson had told him to but, in truth, it was irrelevant where Jamie was playing if he didn't have the ball.

He was in the side to rip opposition defences to shreds with his ferocious speed and intricate skill but, from the very first kick of the game, Jamie knew he wasn't playing as he could. To be at his best on the pitch, his mind had to be clear – focused only on his feet, the ball and the goal. But today Jack was in his head too and there wasn't enough room for everything.

Jamie's legs and whole body seemed drained. On the rare occasions he had the ball, he tried to put his foot on the gas and burn past the Nigeria defenders with his pure, raw pace, only to find that his engine was empty. The nervous energy he'd expended through all the tension before the game seemed to have robbed him of everything he needed now. There was no turbo boost, no jet-propelled dashes down the line.

And he wasn't the only one. The whole team was playing as though they had cement in their boots.

The interval began strangely and did not get much better.

Jamie walked into the dressing room to find Duncan Farrell, the big Scotland striker, smashing his head repeatedly against the wall.

Jamie looked around anxiously. He'd heard that this kind of behaviour was one of the first signs of madness. Had the pressure got to Farrell? Did he need medical help?

But Allie Stone shrugged his shoulders at Jamie and said: "Oh, don't worry about him. He does the same thing every game."

Brian Robertson was also mad. But in a different way. He was mad at his players.

"I want to know if you lot truly believe that you deserve to be playing at the World Cup," he announced. "Because, to me, you look like a bunch of understudies, waiting for the real stars to return... To be the best, you have to *believe* you're the best."

Scotland 0 - 0 Nigeria
70 MINUTES PLAYED

The game went on, but still the spark was missing. Two touches where one would do... Dawdling on the ball and getting caught in possession... Trying to thread the perfect pass through a forest of legs instead of just keeping it simple. These were the symptoms of Scotland's illness.

And, it seemed, the disease was contagious, transmitting itself from the pitch to the stands.

The Tartan Army was getting impatient. The high hopes were turning to loud groans, the big cheers to sarcastic jeers.

And, though he hated to admit it to himself, Jamie knew much of the disappointment was aimed at him. The headlines that had greeted his last-minute decision to play for Scotland had built him up to be such a brilliant player that the Tartan Army were probably just expecting him to turn up and score a hat-trick in his first game. But that was a million miles from the case. Not only had Jamie put in one of the worst performances that he could remember, but a part of his brain wasn't even thinking about football.

Why had Jack ignored him earlier? Hadn't she seen his wave? He swallowed and could still detect the acidic aftertaste of sick on his tongue—

Suddenly a cross was coming over. Jamie was unmarked and the goal was gaping. It was his great chance. All it needed was a good, solid downward header and the goal would be his.

But Jamie had only seen the ball at the last moment. He didn't have enough time to set himself and get into the right position.

The ball hit his head rather than the other way around. The timing was all wrong; Jamie got his head right under the ball, ballooning his effort grotesquely over the crossbar. The Nigerian fans cheered ironically, waving their hands in the air.

Jamie shook his head in self-disgust and jogged back to his station on the left flank.

Still, he consoled himself, a 0-0 draw was not the end of the world. A point and a clean sheet was not the victory that everyone had hoped for, but it was a start. A decent platform from which to build.

And there were still a few minutes left. Jamie could prove his commitment to the fans by working his guts out right until the final whistle. Even if his magic wasn't there today, he could still win people over with his work-rate. Sometimes a sliding tackle earned way more respect than a step-over.

However, although his intentions were good, Jamie's plan to concentrate on his defensive duties was to have utterly disastrous consequences.

With eighty minutes on the clock, the Nigerian

right-winger was leading a bright late break. Jamie decided that *he* was the man to stop the attack.

"Jamie's man!" He roared whilst running back towards his goal at top speed. "I've got him!" With that, Jamie launched himself into what turned out to be a quite horrendously timed tackle.

The winger literally flew five feet into the air and, although he wasn't injured, it was one of the easiest penalties the referee had ever had the fortune to award.

Not even the Tartan Army, who had now gone deathly quiet in the stands, could argue that it wasn't a spot kick.

And although Allie Stone did his best – wiggling his hips and even sticking out his tongue – the Nigerian penalty-taker was having none of it.

He pelted the ball straight into the top corner.

FULL-TIME
Scotland 0 - 1 Nigeria
N Kabu. 81

No points.
No goals.
No clean sheet.
No positives.
GAME OVER.

Jamie hung his head. It was bad enough to have performed so miserably. But now he'd been responsible for gifting the opposition a penalty, which meant that he had almost single-handedly lost Scotland the game.

It was a horrific start and the Tartan Army were not happy. Having been promised by Sir Brian Robertson that they would be following a team capable of winning the tournament, all they could see was a national embarrassment.

And even more criticism rained down from the TV commentators...

"So the disconsolate Scotland players trudge off the pitch and you can see how devastated both the fans and players are by this result. Just look at Jamie Johnson's face. The winger, who was supposed to be the missing ingredient, instead turned out to be the villain.

"This is, after all, the Group of Death and with further tough matches against group rivals France and Argentina looming, it may well be that Scotland's World Cup journey could already be coming to an end.

"This may have been the manager's first taste of World Cup football but it will surely go down as a day of personal humiliation for Sir Brian Robertson and his troops."

Group D – Standings

Teams	Played	For	Against	Points
Argentina	1	2	1	3
Nigeria	1	1	0	3
France	1	1	2	0
Scotland	1	0	1	0

Match Day 1 Results

Argentina 2   -   1 France
M Bertorelli, 32, 88   P Saban, 14

Scotland 0   -   1 Nigeria
N Kabu, 81

⑲ Volunteer Required

"Sorry to interrupt, boss," said Diana Budd, the Scotland Team press officer, poking her head hesitantly around the dressing room door within minutes of the final whistle. "It's TV. That new girl Jack Marshall. She wants to do a post-match interview and they're entitled to one player from each side. We need a volunteer."

All of the players avoided eye contact with her. None of them wanted to have to explain their depressing loss.

Finally, Jamie said: "I'll do it, if you want."

"OK with you, Brian?" checked Diana.

"I don't see many of the other lads putting their hands up," snapped Robertson, still understandably frustrated by the way the game had gone.

"OK, Jamie," said Diana. "Follow me."

*

"Obviously it wasn't the best of games, so some of the questions might be a bit difficult to answer," warned Diana as she led Jamie to the interview area. "A few tips for you. If she asks you about—"

"It's OK, Diana," Jamie smiled. "I know Jack. She won't be like that."

While they were walking, Jamie discreetly checked his breath. He hoped there were no traces of vomit still lingering on it from when he'd been sick before the game. It was strange that, even though she was his best friend, Jack still had the ability to make Jamie feel nervous sometimes. He really cared about what she thought.

As they turned around the corner, Jack was already waiting for them at the bottom of the tunnel which stretched up towards the pitch. She was standing in front of a board with various sponsors' names on it.

"Hey, Jack," smiled Jamie, resisting the urge to give her a hug. "I waved at you before the game but I don't think you s—"

Jack put her fingers to her lips to silence Jamie before holding the microphone to her mouth and, in a loud voice, announcing: "Thanks, Jeff. Yes, I'm joined here by Jamie Johnson. So, Jamie, tell us: where did it all go wrong?"

Jamie looked at her face. It was cold and serious. Her smile was nowhere to be seen.

"Well, I don't think that anything went wrong as such..." Jamie stammered.

"Well, presumably something must have gone wrong," Jack persisted. "Our stats showed that Scotland only had three efforts on goal during the game, with just one on target. Would you put that down to the manager's tactics or the players' performances?"

"Well, I don't think anyone's to blame but, when the whistle goes, we're the ones who go out on to the pitch – not the manager."

"And what about your own relationship with the fans? Are you still sure you made the right decision picking Scotland? It seems like the Tartan Army haven't accepted you yet. They weren't exactly cheering your name."

Jamie's mouth hung open. Was this his friend? Was this his best friend? Or had some repugnant alien killed Jack and hijacked her body?

"The fans can do what they want," Jamie snapped, firing out the words without understanding their impact. "I couldn't care less."

⑳
On the Net

Jamie went straight up to his room. The coach back to the hotel had been as silent as a morgue. Stonefish hadn't had the will to break the silence with even the softest of farts.

WORLD CUP WALL CHART

Group A Fixtures/Results

Date	Fixture		
11th Jun	Sth Africa /	– /	Chile
11th Jun	Portugal ◌	– ◌	Morocco
16th Jun	Sth Africa	–	Portugal
17th Jun	Morocco	–	Chile
22nd Jun	Chile	–	Portugal
22nd Jun	Morocco	–	Sth Africa

Group B Fixtures/Results

Date	Fixture		
12th Jun	Sth Korea 2	– ◌	Greece
12th Jun	Germany /	– ◌	Australia
17th Jun	Germany	–	Sth Korea
17th Jun	Greece	–	Australia
22nd Jun	Australia	–	Sth Korea
22nd Jun	Greece	–	Germany

Group C Fixtures/Results

Date	Fixture		
12th Jun	Russia /	– /	Brazil
13th Jun	Iraq ◌	– /	USA
18th Jun	USA	–	Brazil
18th Jun	Russia	–	Iraq
23rd Jun	USA	–	Russia
23rd Jun	Brazil	–	Iraq

Group D Fixtures/Results

Date	Fixture		
13th Jun	Scotland ◌	– /	Nigeria
13th Jun	Argentina 2	– /	France
18th Jun	France	–	Scotland
18th Jun	Nigeria	–	Argentina
23rd Jun	France	–	Nigeria
23rd Jun	Scotland	–	Argentina

Group E Fixtures/Results

Date	Fixture		
14th Jun	Spain	–	Canada
14th Jun	Ivory Coast	–	Denmark
19th Jun	Spain	–	Ivory Coast
19th Jun	Denmark	–	Canada
24th Jun	Canada	–	Ivory Coast
24th Jun	Denmark	–	Spain

Group F Fixtures/Results

Date	Fixture		
14th Jun	Egypt	–	Turkey
15th Jun	Belgium	–	England
20th Jun	England	–	Turkey
20th Jun	Egypt	–	Belgium
24th Jun	England	–	Egypt
24th Jun	Turkey	–	Belgium

Group G Fixtures/Results

Date	Fixture		
14th Jun	Honduras	–	Japan
15th Jun	Italy	–	Switzerland
20th Jun	Italy	–	Honduras
20th Jun	Japan	–	Switzerland
24th Jun	Switzerland	–	Honduras
24th Jun	Japan	–	Italy

Group H Fixtures/Results

Date	Fixture		
16th Jun	Croatia	–	Norway
16th Jun	Holland	–	Cameroon
21st Jun	Norway	–	Cameroon
21st Jun	Holland	–	Croatia
25th Jun	Cameroon	–	Croatia
25th Jun	Norway	–	Holland

Jamie reluctantly filled in the scores on his wall chart before checking all the footy stories on the internet through his phone. As the page loaded, his already sinking heart plummeted to new depths of depression.

Footy Blogs

Marshall Mauls Clueless Johnson

Scotland winger Jamie Johnson capped a miserable international debut this afternoon when he was grilled live on TV by his girlfriend, Jack Marshall.

The 18-year-old star failed to live up to his pre-match billing as one of the most dangerous attackers in the tournament – and even conceded the late penalty which consigned his team to defeat – before being subjected to an embarrassing barrage of questions by the rising sports reporter.

When Johnson – who came so close to playing for England – was asked about his frosty relationship with the Scotland fans, he snapped: "I couldn't care less."

Onlookers at the match said that Johnson had even appeared to be distracted during the game itself, with one theory being that he had been put off by Marshall's pitch-side presence.

It raises questions about whether he has the mental strength to focus on his football when his girlfriend is close at hand.

One thing is certain, Johnson will be hoping the French defenders are easier opponents than Marshall, who showed that she will pull no punches during her coverage of the tournament.

YOUR SAY

So what is the reason for Johnson's woeful form?

VOTE NOW:

Put off by Jack Marshall 45%

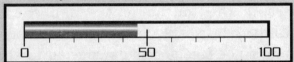

Not good enough to play at a World Cup 34%

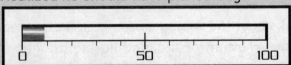

Realized he should have picked England 9%

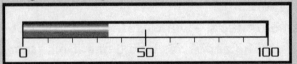

Who knows! 12%

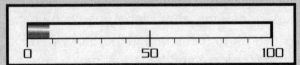

6 Comments:

I'm not surprised he was put off by JM. She is lush! She can interview me anytime!

Barry, Bushey, 6.34 p.m.

Well said, Neil! Johnson was rubbish. Thought he was supposed to be a good passer. Didn't look like he could pass wind to me!

Hamish, Dundee, 6.09 p.m.

Bring back Treach. He never let Scotland down. Johnson saying he "couldn't care less" was a disgrace. Not surprised, though – he didn't even sing the national anthem. He's just dirty scum. We don't need that sort of player.

Neil, Clydebank, 6.01 p.m.

Forget Johnson. He ain't the prob. Everything in football's about the manager. What's Robertson on? Tactics were awful and how did he pick that team?! He couldn't pick his nose. Korea looked a hundred times better than us last night.

Alec, 5.49 p.m.

We should drop Johnson. What was that tackle

for their penalty?! Are we sure he's not been sent to us by the English to get us knocked out?! I counted – he only touched the ball five times. And most of them were in the warm-up!

Gregor, Ayr, 5.28 p.m.

OMG! Just watched Jamie Johnson interview on TV. Guy speaks worse than he plays! He's a joke!

Dougie, Kilmarnock , 5.13 p.m.

"Hi, JJ, how you doing?" said Jack, answering her phone. Suddenly she sounded like herself again. Like the real Jack, not the alien Jack. Not that Jamie was going to allow her to get off that easily.

"How am I doing?" he snarled. "How am I doing?! Erm, well, let's see… I had an absolute mare and then got hammered live on TV by … let me think, oh yeah, that's right, by you! Thanks for that, Jack!"

He spat out her name with a viciousness that shocked both of them. Jack didn't say anything in response.

"Why did you do that, Jack? Why?" he growled.

"Sorry, Jamie," she responded, colder now. "But what did you expect me to do? Say you were amazing?! I've got to ask the questions that need to be asked. That's my job."

"So what is your job, then? To mug me off and make me look like an idiot on TV?"

"Get a grip, Jamie."

"No, I've got a better idea," Jamie barked. "YOU get a grip!"

And without bothering to hang up, Jamie just chucked his phone at the wall, instantly smashing it into pieces.

㉑
Live For Ever

Jamie was in a foul, filthy mood.

Not only had he just had another two threatening phone calls come through to his room, but a series of dark questions and doubts were beginning to seep through his brain like a black stain.

He was upset, furious even, with Jack for making him look stupid on TV. He was also angry at himself for falsely assuming that it would be so easy for him to be accepted as a Scotland player. What had he ever done for Scotland, apart from give away a stupid goal against Nigeria? Now at least the England fans and the Scotland fans had something in common: they both hated Jamie Johnson.

But neither of those issues, however, was his real

problem. There was another deeper, more damning realization that was gnawing away at him. He tried to dismiss it, but like a painful ulcer, it stayed there, throbbing malignantly.

The truth was that maybe Jamie had gone as far as he could go as a footballer. He'd been the star at school, he'd shone at academy level, and he'd already proved himself in the Premier League. But maybe international football – the World Cup finals – was one step too far for him.

Suddenly Jamie's thoughts were interrupted once again by the phone's aggressive ringing. But, with his career in freefall and millions of people hating him, Bertorelli had picked the wrong time to start messing with Jamie.

As he angrily picked up the receiver, all of Jamie's fears and frustrations were translated into the volume of his voice as he roared down the phone: "Now you listen to me, YOU STUPID…"

"I don't know who you think you're talking to," said the unmistakeable voice of Sir Brian Robertson on the other end of the line. "But I want to see you in my office. Now."

"Where's he gone then?" asked Robertson.

He and Jamie were sitting across the desk from each

other in the manager's office that had been set up in the hotel. Robertson had his glasses on. He looked serious. And concerned.

"Who?" asked Jamie.

"The final piece of my jigsaw. The key to my team. Where's he gone?"

"I don't know," sighed Jamie. He had so many questions and doubts swirling around in his mind and they seemed to be doubling by the second. "It was just so different out there tonight; so tight, so tactical... Maybe I'm not clever enough for it … or maybe I'm just not good enough."

"Not good enough?" Robertson repeated, his eyes almost popping out of his head. "Not good enough?! Jamie, you are – how can I put this without giving you too big a head? You are a once-in-a-generation talent. You're the type of player that granddads tell their grandkids about. You're the type of player … whose name should live for ever."

Jamie felt his palms glisten with sweat. Hearing those words had sent a chill running down his spine.

"Cheers," said Jamie, shifting a little uneasily in his seat.

"You don't like it when people say nice things about you, do you, Jamie." Robertson smiled. "Why is that, do you think?"

Jamie shrugged his shoulders. "I don't know," he said. "Sometimes it's easier when people just tell me what I've done wrong."

"Well, when you do something wrong, believe me I'll tell you. Until then, I want you to forget the idea that you're not up to international level. I believe in you. Totally. And in return, you can be honest with me and tell me what's really up. Look at you. You look awful, those bags under your eyes. Have you slept since you've got here?"

"Not much," admitted Jamie. He thought for a second about whether he should tell Sir Brian what had been happening and quickly came to the conclusion that, right now, he had very little to lose.

"I've been getting some funny phone calls," Jamie said, almost apologetically. "To my room, late at night, heavy breathing and all that stuff. I mean, it's probably just Bertorelli trying to wind me up – I know he's got a problem with me and I'm not scared of him, but still, it gets to you after a while."

"Yes, I can imagine it does," said Sir Brian Robertson, standing up and moving around his desk as if he had somewhere to go. "Especially at a World Cup... And you say all these calls have been direct to your room, none on your mobile?"

Jamie nodded.

"Well, now it makes sense. I wish you'd told me earlier, you know," said Robertson, shaking his head. "No one can be expected to play if they can't sleep…All right, well, I know *now* and I know what I have to do."

"OK, boss," said Jamie, slowly getting out of his chair. He understood what Robertson was saying and he could hardly argue; it was time for him to go – in more ways than one.

"Jamie," said Brian Robertson, as Jamie was about to open the door. "Don't blame yourself. It's not your fault."

"OK," said Jamie, though it was hardly much of a consolation. He had an ominous feeling. He knew what was about to happen next.

Robertson nodded gravely. "You can close the door behind you, Jamie."

22

Making the Change

An air of tension filled the room. It was 11 p.m. and the entire squad – some of whom had been asleep – had been called out of their rooms to attend an urgent team meeting.

This was highly unusual and everyone knew it. Something serious was about to go down.

"You're probably wondering why you're here," announced Sir Brian Robertson reading his players' minds. "Well, I'm not happy. Not happy with the performance against Nigeria, not happy with the result, and most of all, I'm not happy with the spirit in the camp. I'm not the kind of bloke that mucks around, so I'm going to make a change. Now."

The players looked at one another like a herd of

antelope suddenly aware that they had been stalked by a hungry lion. Someone was going to be sacrificed. The question was: who?

Jamie felt the butterflies rise in his chest. He had a pretty good idea who was going to be dropped.

"I'm going to make a change in the left wing position," Robertson said, confirming Jamie's fears.

Robertson paused before continuing.

"What do you think about that, Ronnie?" he asked Ronnie Treacher.

"Well … boss … that's your call … but if you want me to play … obviously I won't say no."

Of course you won't, Jamie thought to himself, *you suck up*.

"Yes, I thought not," said Robertson, before turning to look Treacher in the eye. "So is that why you've been making threatening phone calls to Jamie's room?"

Suddenly all the players turned to face Treacher, including Jamie.

"What?" said Treacher, his face filling with colour. "I don't know what you—"

"Be very careful before you deny it, Ronnie," warned Robertson. "I've spoken to reception and I have the records of all the calls made from your room. So I'll ask you again: why did you make the calls?"

Silence. A bead of sweat rolled down Treacher's

forehead, dripping on to his shirt.

"Just a bit of fun," he said, attempting to squeeze out an uncomfortable smile. "Only a bit of banter, you know, him being the new boy and everything. Ask the lads. We always have a bit of fun with the new players."

Robertson nodded and then calmly said, "OK, Ronnie, you're done. Go and pack your bags."

"What? You're joking, gaffer. I've played for this team for twelve years. And now you're going to drop me for phoning his room? You can't even call up a replacement. You're having a laugh, aren't you?"

"Look at my face," said Robertson, his expression as hard as steel. "Do I look like I'm joking? Don't worry, we'll spare your blushes. I'll tell the press you tore a hamstring in training. Now get your stuff and go. A taxi's waiting for you outside."

Ronnie Treacher stood up and walked towards the door.

"This is your fault," he turned to shout at Jamie. "You should have stayed with England. You don't belong here. You'll never be one of us!"

And with that, he slammed the door behind him.

Sir Brian Robertson let his players take in what had just happened. Then he addressed them once more.

"We're all new to one another," he said. "So perhaps

I need to get a couple of things straight. One, I don't give a monkey's how it worked before I got here. Two, all of my teams are a unit. We play together, we work together and we support one another, no matter what happens or who's playing.

"Stick to those rules and we'll be OK... And three, everyone, and I mean *everyone*, sings the national anthem before the game. If you don't know the words, THEN LEARN THEM.

"OK," he said, suddenly lightening his tone. "Meeting over. See you for training in the morning."

With the execution now complete, the room began to empty. As the players filed out like schoolboys after assembly, a hush of total and utter respect accompanied them. An energy filled the air as they contemplated the swiftness and confidence with which Robertson had taken such a big decision.

And in their own minds, all of the players were coming to the same realization. If they hadn't already suspected it, there could now be no doubt – in Sir Brian Robertson they had a proper manager on their hands. Someone to be truly reckoned with.

After a couple of minutes, only Jamie and Sir Brain remained in the room. It was Jamie who broke the silence.

"Boss, how did you—?"

But before he could finish, Robertson said, "You can't dial straight to our rooms from outside the hotel. You have to come through reception and they have been told not to put calls through. Only someone else in the hotel could have called you in your room."

"Oh," replied Jamie, beginning to piece it together in his mind. "Right... Well, thanks."

"I won't regret it," said Robertson. "Now go and get some sleep. You need it."

23

Weight of Expectation

Sunday 17 June – the day before Scotland's second group game v France

Jamie looked down at his bulging thighs before exhaling and pushing with all his might. His muscles strained and shook but he pushed harder. He believed he could lift that weight – he *told* himself he could. Then, with a huge, final heave, his feet and legs lifted the massive block of weights. He held it there for five full seconds before letting it crash back down with a loud clank.

Beneath the large, worm-like scar that snaked all the way across his knee, Jamie could feel the blood rushing through his joints and muscles. If he tensed his thighs now they might burst through his shorts. He had spent hundreds of hours building up the muscles around his knee so that they would be strong enough to bear the strain of his playing top level football.

It was amazing to think that a metal plate and set of screws were all that was holding his knee together. After the car accident at Foxborough, all the doctors had told him he'd never play again, but with Archie's help he'd proved them all wrong when he'd made his comeback at Hawkstone. True, his knee would never be completely right again but that just made Jamie even more determined to work as hard as he could in the gym to stay in the best condition possible. It was the only way.

Pace *and* strength. Jamie knew he needed both for this tournament. One wouldn't be enough. It had to be both.

He stood up and rubbed his biceps. He was now halfway through his daily gym session. He'd done his legs and chest. Now it was time for his arms. As he went to pick up a heavy dumb-bell, Jamie saw Sir Brian Robertson come up on the big TV screen in the gym.

He turned up the volume.

"Yes, there were a few grumbles from our fans at the end of our last game," Robertson was saying to a packed press conference. "And they're entitled to that – I would have felt the same if I'd been in the crowd.

Our spirit wasn't right in that game, but I'm confident that it is now."

Jamie nodded as he curled the dumb-bell up towards his shoulder, feeling his bicep tighten and rise in response. Since the incident with Treacher and the way the manager had handled it, a new invigoration and harmony had swept around the squad. It was as though, in that moment, Robertson had stamped his authority on the players and now they were completely in his hold.

One of the most impressive aspects of Robertson's style was his man management. He knew exactly how to treat each player. When dealing with rebellious centre forward Duncan Farrell, for example, Robertson would often be a little more lenient, as if he were dealing with a naughty but talented schoolboy. Meanwhile, with Jamie, he kept his instructions simple and encouraging, often taking his winger aside for a little chat.

Robertson had not mentioned Jamie's terrible tackle that had given away a penalty against Nigeria for four full days. Then this morning he'd approached Jamie at breakfast and said gently: "Do me a favour, son. Stop messing around in our penalty area, will you? Get up the other end. That's why you're in the side."

*

"Brian, looking at the make-up of your squad, if Ronnie Treacher's hamstring is that bad that it keeps him out for the whole tournament, that leaves you with just Jamie Johnson as your only recognized left-winger," one journalist was commenting in the pre-match press conference. "That must be a bit of a problem because, after his performance against Nigeria and what he said about the fans after the match, you must be tempted to drop Johnson for the France game."

"Eh, laddie," snapped Robertson. "How about you leave the management to me? Jamie Johnson is a humble lad. Yes, he's got fire in his belly, but he's been brought up with values. He'll win the fans over. He just needs a bit more time – that's all."

"But isn't time the one luxury you don't have, Sir Brian?" the journalist responded. "You need a win against France or you're as good as out. Do you think he'll be ready in time for tomorrow? And isn't it about character, too? Are you convinced he has got the courage and the temperament to do it at this level?"

"Courage? Temperament?!" Robertson said, visibly riled now. "You try having a steel plate inserted in your knee and being told your career is over when you're fifteen! Has Jamie Johnson got the character to play at the World Cup? Will he be ready?" Robertson fixed the journalist with his steely stare. "I'd bet my house on it."

Still watching the TV, Jamie roared aloud as he raised the biggest weight he'd ever lifted. He'd be ready by tomorrow all right.

A Point
to Prove

Monday 18 June – Match Day

GROUP D
France v Scotland
Emirates Stadium
KICK-OFF 3 p.m.

If Scotland had thought that it was going to be any easier for them against France, then they were quickly corrected by the opening ten minutes of this vital encounter.

The French unit seemed to be almost the perfect blend. Half of their team comprised big, strong and quick athletes, and they were the ideal complement to the nimble little ball players that played alongside them.

The playmakers in their team had been dubbed "*Les Artistes*" by the French press, and it was easy to see why, as they painted pretty patterns with the ball.

The French came out of the traps bursting with imagination and confidence. Their comfort and ease at playing at this level served only to further highlight Scotland's own lack of World Cup experience. At times it resembled kids playing against adults.

The lightning-quick break which resulted in France's opening goal was a lesson in clinical, modern football. Their winger, Tapin, exchanged passes before carrying the ball twenty yards forward and laying it into their striker, Santini, who was lurking on the edge of the box like a hungry fox.

Santini controlled the ball instantly and turned in order to return the ball to Tapin. Yet when he saw that the entire Scotland defence was concerned with Tapin, he simply wrong-footed them with a neat drag-back on the half-turn, earning himself just enough time and space to rifle the ball right into the very top corner of the net.

With three back flips and a series of high fives to celebrate, France were on their way. Scotland, meanwhile, were in complete disarray.

*

France 1 - 0 Scotland
J Santini. 8

"Hold the ball! Calm down!" Sir Brian Robertson implored to his players from the touchline, immediately sensing the panic that was taking hold in his team. Every pass looked under pressure, every kick seemed clumsy. They were playing fast, frenzied football, when what they really needed was a touch of class and composure.

If they could just get through to half-time without conceding another goal, then Robertson might be able to get into their heads, organize them, inject some belief back into their play.

Thankfully, the players heeded Robertson's advice and managed to gain a foothold in the game by at least stringing a few passes together.

Which was why it came as an almighty blow when, on the brink of half-time, the France centre-half was allowed to advance, unchallenged, as far as the edge of the Scotland area. With few other options open to him, he got his head down and unleashed an effort at goal.

It was a stinging strike but it was sailing straight into Allie Stone's welcoming arms – until it took a freakish flick off the back of Cameron McManus's heel, causing it to veer sharply into the air and somehow loop over

Allie Stone and into the back of the net.

France 2   -   0 Scotland
J Santini, 8
F Loufour, 43

"*Allez les Bleus!*" roared the French fans from all around the ground.

At first, the Scotland section of the ground was as silent as a cemetery. They knew they were witnessing the death of their World Cup dreams.

But then, watching Robertson lead his men down the tunnel for half-time, the Tartan Army's disapproval metamorphosed into a murmur, grew into a grumble and finally forced itself into a fully fledged roar:

"YOU DON'T KNOW WHAT YOU'RE DOING! YOU DON'T KNOW WHAT YOU'RE DOING!"

They yelled angrily at their manager. Indeed, some of the fans, disgusted by Scotland's performance, had already seen enough and were leaving the ground, even though it was only half-time.

"Go back to England, Johnson!" shouted one furious-looking man at Jamie. The fan, who was bare-chested and heavily tattooed, was storming out of the stadium in anger. But not before he'd told Jamie what he really thought of him.

"You're not one of us," he continued viciously, each word of his vitriol laced with pure aggression. "We'll never like you – ever!"

Nothing hurt Jamie more than being abused by his own fans. It was the worst feeling in football. And what made it all the more painful was that he agreed with them – right now Jamie hated himself.

France 2 - 0 Scotland
J Santini. 8
F Loufour. 43
HALF-TIME

Trailing by two, Scotland had much to do, so Brian Robertson's half-time instructions were short and to the point.

"One chance," he said, gravely. "You'll probably only have *one chance* to play in a World Cup in your entire careers. Is this how you want to go out of it? Is it? Without even trying? Without even showing what you're capable of?

"Losing inspires winners and it defeats losers. So, which one are we – winners or losers? You've got forty-five minutes left of this game to prove that you are winners, gentlemen. If I were you, I'd give it every last thing I had because, believe me, if you don't, you'll regret it for the rest of your lives."

Jamie and his teammates took in every word and solemnly rose to their feet to get back out there. Right now, they were at rock bottom, but one goal was all they needed to get back into this game. One goal could change everything.

While Duncan Farrell psyched himself up by hammering the wall with his head, Robertson pulled Jamie aside for a quick chat.

"Don't worry about what those French players were saying about you," Robertson whispered discreetly to Jamie. "It's a lack of respect on their part. You just play your normal game."

"What do you mean?" asked Jamie, confused. "Who was saying what about me?"

"The stuff they were saying about you being rubbish and overrated. Ignore them; they're just trying to wind you up."

At first, Jamie was stunned. But then he began to feel the anger rising from the soles of his feet. Overrated? Easy to play against? Jamie could feel his teeth grinding together and his jaw jutting out aggressively.

Now, Jamie had a point to prove. And he wanted to prove it immediately.

Game On

France 2 - 0 Scotland
J Santini, 8
F Loufour, 43
SECOND-HALF

As the referee blew loudly on his whistle to restart the game, the noise was drowned out in Jamie's mind by a series of words which were being repeated with such an insistent rhythm that they sounded almost like a song.

I'll show them! These feet can do anything with a football… These feet can do anything with a football…

He heard the words over and over again and he recognized the voice as his own.

And just then, like a faithful lost dog happily returning to its owner, the ball came back to Jamie.

Jamie collected it comfortably into his stride and set off like a rocket. He felt himself smoothly accelerating into his turbo gear as he drove deeper and deeper into French territory. These fools had said Jamie was overrated. Now they were going to pay.

Scared and shocked by the sudden show of electric pace, the French defence seemed to melt and part in front of Jamie, inviting him to go on yet further.

With a final, gravity-defying dummy, he waltzed past the last defender and tore towards the byline, where he smashed the ball across the turf.

Running back towards his own goal, the French defender could feel Duncan Farrell's menacing presence behind him. Aware that Farrell was arriving just in time to slot the ball home, the French defender had no option but to make sure he met Jamie's centre first and try to lift the ball over the goal. But the cross was too powerfully hit to control, meaning the defender could do nothing other than volley the ball straight into his own net. In a flash it was in, smashing its way into the back of the net.

Jamie had created a goal, the Tartan Army had something to cheer about and at long last Scotland were back in the game.

Jamie sprinted over to the Scotland bench and gave his manager a high five.

"Boss," he said, still panting from his pitch-long run to the byline. "You know what you said yesterday … in the press conference … about me showing people what I've got when I'm ready?"

Robertson nodded.

"Well, guess what? I'm ready."

France 2 - 1 Scotland
J Santini. 8   C Cougier. 06. 51
F Loufour. 43
SECOND-HALF

While the French team reorganized themselves and put the ball back on the centre spot, Jamie inhaled a deep breath and tilted his head back to look at the sky. A bird, he could not make out which type, was flying freely and gracefully from one side of the stadium roof to the other. It picked up speed as it weaved and dipped through the air. Jamie smiled. That's how he felt when he played his best football – free as a bird.

With time beginning to ebb away, Scotland were still behind. The afternoon was turning to evening and the dark danger of Scotland's exit from the tournament began to loom ever larger.

As the last of the afternoon sunlight tickled Jamie's cheeks, he knew that now was the moment for him to step out of the shadows.

There were less than thirty minutes remaining when, using his anticipation to read a French passing move, Jamie swooped to intercept a loose ball in the centre circle.

He had possession. He felt free. It was time for him to fly.

Jamie soared across the ground, his feet barely touching the turf. Then, as a French midfielder advanced, Jamie did something truly remarkable.

He trapped the ball behind his heel and looped it over both his and the French defender's head with a rainbow flick! It was an astonishing, breathtaking piece of artistry.

But Jamie wasn't finished there. He skipped around the defender and he watched the ball drop towards his left foot before executing a volley with such sweet perfection that it roared towards the goal.

Jamie was forty yards out, so he followed right through his strike to get the maximum amount of power and momentum. Then he watched, transfixed like everyone else in the ground, as the ball arrowed towards the target. It shot through the air like a bullet, dipping at the very last moment just enough to kiss the underside of the crossbar on its way into the back of the net.

For just a second the entire stadium was in silence

… sixty thousand fans were frozen into paralysis by a moment of pure footballing genius… And then a blast of such huge noise erupted that it shook the ground to its very foundations.

France 2	-	2 Scotland
J Santini, 8		C Cougier, 06, 51
F Loufour, 43		J Johnson, 65

It had finally dawned on Sir Brian Robertson's side that they had what it took to mix it with the very best. They deserved their place at football's top table.

Meanwhile, their star player felt light on his feet, powerful in his mind, and dangerous with the ball. He was hungry for another helping.

With confidence now coursing through his veins, Jamie went on dribble after dribble, constantly teasing the French defenders into committing to the tackle before flicking it past them and skipping away. His pace was extraordinary. He seemed to have a change of gear, even when he appeared to already be running at top speed. It was just the same as when he used to play Tag in the playground. Once Jamie got away from someone, they were never going to catch him. Ever.

And, almost like a brother who didn't want his sibling rival to steal all the attention, Duncan Farrell quickly made sure that he got in on the act too.

In the seventy-third minute, he went up for a Jamie Johnson cross and bulldozed his way through the French defence to head the ball home. The dejected French keeper protested that he had been pushed out of the way, but the fact was he had simply been outmuscled by the fearsome Scotland striker.

France 2 - 3 Scotland
J Santini. 8   C Cougier. 06. 51
F Loufour. 43   J Johnson. 65
                 D Farrell. 73

Then with six minutes remaining, Farrell latched on to another killer pass from Jamie before belting in Scotland's fourth from way outside the area.

It was a strike of quite ballistic proportions. It seemed to travel the twenty-five yards to the goal faster than the speed of sound because it crashed into the back of the net almost before you could hear the noise of Farrell's size thirteen boot smashing into the ball. Never had Jamie seen a shot hit so hard.

France 2 - 4 Scotland
J Santini. 8   C Cougier. 06. 51
F Loufour. 43   J Johnson. 65
                 D Farrell. 73. 84

On any other day, Farrell's second strike would have been goal of the match, but today there was only going to be one recipient of that prize.

At the end of the game Jamie went over to the Tartan Army to throw his shirt into the crowd. It started an almighty scramble. Grown men were acting like kids, pushing and pulling to try to get their hands on the shirt. Some of them were even pulling one another's hair!

Forty-five minutes before, fans were ready to leave the ground, angry, blaming Jamie for the death of their World Cup hopes.

The fans were still going mental, but now they were shouting Jamie's name with pride and dramatically bowing in front of him.

Both the players and fans knew that finally, at long last, and just at the right time, Scotland had pulled out a performance. Their World Cup campaign was up and running. And their magic man had started to weave his special spell on the tournament.

FULL-TIME		
France 2	-	4 Scotland
J Santini. 8		C Cougier. 06. 51
F Loufour. 43		J Johnson. 65
		D Farrell. 73. 84

Brian Robertson was in a jubilant mood in the dressing room when the players got back.

"Now that is what I call a second-half performance," he beamed, slapping every player on the back. "You lot were superb! By the way, when we get back to the hotel, we're having a quiz night. And the good news is you can eat whatever you want!"

The players bellowed their approval. They had been begging the manager for something different to eat after all the grilled fish and pasta they had been force-fed over the last few days.

"A cheeseburger! Beauty!" yelled Duncan Farrell.

"Chips!" shrieked Pat Renton, the full-back.

"Yeah! And extra baked beans!" added Allie Stone.

Meanwhile, in the corner of the dressing room, Jamie quietly collected his ring from Tommy the kit man and slipped it back on. He'd be after some Chinese tonight.

"Nice goal, son," said Brian Robertson, approaching Jamie. "But I don't ever want to see you doing that again."

"Doing what?" asked a bewildered Jamie. He'd never been told off for scoring a goal before.

"It's a good skill. I'll give you that. And it's fine for showing off. But you don't use flicks like that in a game. It winds up the opposition. Trust me. I know what I'm talking about."

"But I was angry, boss. I did the rainbow flick cos I wanted to show those French defenders what I could do after what they'd said about me. I wanted to prove them wrong."

This time it was Brian Robertson's turn to look confused.

"They said that I was rubbish and that I didn't even deserve to be playing at the World Cup. Remember? You told me at half-time."

"Oh, Jamie." Robertson smiled almost sympathetically. "Did I ever tell you? I don't speak a word of French."

Group D – Standings

Teams	Played	For	Against	Points
Argentina	2	5	1	6
Scotland	2	4	3	3
Nigeria	2	1	3	3
France	2	3	6	0

Match Day 2 Results

Argentina 3 - 0 Nigeria
M Bertorelli, 13, 27
P Hurrico, 69

France 2 - 4 Scotland
J Santini, 8   C Cougier, 06, 51
F Loufour, 43   J Johnson, 65
                    D Farrell, 73, 84

Final Matches Remaining in Group D

Match Day 3
23 June
France v Nigeria KICK-OFF 3 p.m.
Scotland v Argentina KICK-OFF 8 p.m.

26
BFG

She hadn't been there.

On his big day, on the day he'd scored the goal of his life. She had been nowhere to be seen.

So where had she been?

Jamie only had to turn on his TV to get the answer.

There Jack was, looking annoyingly happy, hosting live coverage of England's training session ahead of their crunch Group F game against Turkey. She was standing between two of the England players, wishing them luck for their big game.

The players were bare-chested. They were smiling at her, while she praised their individual qualities as though she was their personal cheerleader. It was sickening.

Turning off the TV in disgust, Jamie slammed his door shut behind him and stomped down the hotel stairs. He felt as if someone had stabbed him in the stomach and twisted the knife.

He was in no mood for a quiz night.

"Big Fatty...?!" repeated Allie Stone, literally shrieking with laughter. He was stamping his feet on the ground in hysterics. "Big Fatty..."

Each time he tried to begin the sentence, he got through a couple of words before descending again into hysterical laughter, which, after a while, transformed into a coughing fit.

"It's not that funny," said Jamie. "Just cos you knew what 'flatulent' meant doesn't make you some kind of genius all of a sudden. Just drop it now, will you?"

"Oh, but it *is* that funny!" said Stonefish, starting up again. "Big Fatty—"

"All right!" snapped Jamie. "I got one answer wrong, so what?! Do you have to keep on laughing about it?"

"Yeah, but there's getting it wrong and getting it *wrong*, isn't there? I mean, even I know what BFG stands for and I haven't read a book for about twenty years! I mean, you gotta tell me, where did you get Big Fatty Goat from?! What kind of books do *you* read? Hey, Jamie, where are you going? Come back! I wanna know what you think the OMG stands for!"

Jamie had had enough. The whole room had cracked up when he'd got the answer wrong. Even the players on his team. Big Fatty Goat! What had he been thinking? If he didn't know the answer he should have just kept quiet.

He sat down by himself in the hotel lobby and miserably spun his ring on the table in front of him. With his mobile broken and his new one not yet delivered, he couldn't even pretend he was texting, which was what he normally did if he was ever in a restaurant by himself and didn't want to look sad.

As his ring spun, so did Jamie's mind. He hated seeing Jack talking to other players, but he knew she would say she was just doing "her job". But why wasn't it her job to interview him about the best goal he'd ever scored—

"Excuse me," said a voice from behind Jamie.

Jamie turned around to see a girl – a really pretty girl – smiling broadly at him. She had sparkling blue eyes and very blonde hair. Jamie immediately recognized her as the hairdresser in the hotel.

"Sorry to interrupt you, but I'm a really big fan of yours," said the girl, who had very long eyelashes and was wearing quite a bit of make-up. "Could I have my photo taken with you, please?"

"Sure," replied, Jamie a little too eagerly. He'd completely forgotten everything he was thinking about and for some reason his voice had gone really high, too. It sounded as it had done when he was ten!

If he was honest, Jamie still had no idea what to say to girls. On the pitch, he could produce a rainbow flick goal to defeat international-class defenders. Off the pitch, when faced with a pretty girl, he struggled to muster a hello.

"I'm Loretta, by the way," said the girl, pushing herself really close to Jamie as she reached her phone in front of them to take a picture. "But you can call me Lolly."

Jamie tried to reproduce his "cool" smile that he'd practised hundreds of times in the mirror.

He stared at the camera, concentrating on tensing his cheeks at the right time.

But while he was focusing on getting his look right, Loretta did something that took Jamie completely by surprise.

Just as the flash went off, she quickly leaned her lips into his cheek and gave him a kiss!

㉗
Big Story

FOOTBALL

CharlesSummers
at the Emirates

Best Goal Ever?

As a journalist, you don't record the time of the goal Jamie Johnson scored at the Emirates yesterday. You simply remember the date. To score from just over the halfway line is one thing. But to do so on the volley, from your own rainbow flick, is quite something else. Perhaps a one-in-a-million shot – and this was at a time when many, arguably even Johnson himself, were questioning whether he had what it took to play at the very highest level.

Of course, we should ward against going over the top in our praise of Johnson's strike. It is entirely possible that this was not the best goal ever scored. However, if it wasn't, I for one would like to see the strike that was.

Match Ratings out of Ten

Stone 8, Renton 7, Miller 7, Nixon 8, Tulley 7, McManus 7,
Baxter 6, McCall 7, Farrell 8, Gray 7, Johnson 9

Man of the Match: Jamie Johnson

Awesome second-half display, topped by the rainbow
flick goal. How many players in the world could do that?

Want to learn the skill? See below for our instructions.

1. Step over the ball
with your leading foot.

2. Lock the ball against the
back of your leading foot with
the inside of your rear foot.

4. Flick your leading foot back, kicking the ball over your head with your heel.

3. With your rear foot roll the ball up your leg about 10cm.

5. Land on your other foot and continue running to meet the ball as it hits the ground.

Jamie smiled. He'd had every single paper delivered to his room. And he hadn't been disappointed. He was on practically every back page. As always, he read Charles Summers' report first. He didn't always understand every word Summers wrote, but he liked the descriptions he used. Sometimes it sounded almost like poetry. If Jamie had been good at English instead of football, he would have liked to have been a football writer as good as Charles Summers.

But probably the best part of all was the fact that, beneath Charles Summers' report, the newspaper had employed an illustrator to recreate Jamie's rainbow flick, to show kids at home how to do it themselves!

Jamie gave the newspaper ten out of ten for putting in those illustrations. He still practised his skills every day, so he liked the thought of kids up and down the country going out to work on their own rainbow flicks. He'd like to know if Robbie Simmonds could do that!

Jamie started to cut some of the reports out of the papers. His mum was away and he knew she'd want him to keep them for her folder. At home she'd kept all the articles that had ever been written about him, going right back to the ones from the local newspaper when he was still at school. Jamie suspected that she'd probably missed his goal against France anyway – she had an unfortunate habit of somehow always managing to be in the toilet whenever Jamie scored!

He was just throwing away the rest of the papers when he thought he saw someone that looked like him on the front page of one of the tabloids.

Jamie looked closer and could not believe what he saw. It *was* him.

NEW GIRL for WING WIZARD

Perfect

WORLD CUP *Match*

Star of the moment Jamie Johnson found the perfect way to celebrate his Man of the Match performance against France – by making a new friend.

Johnson, whose fresh-faced good looks have the potential to make him the pin-up boy of the tournament, had been rumoured to be seeing his childhood sweetheart, TV reporter Jacqueline Marshall. But, as this picture shows, he is clearly ready to make a substitution off the field.

The blonde beauty pictured with Johnson is part-time model Loretta Martin.

"We were both staying in the hotel and we just got chatting," stunning 19-year-old, Martin, told us.

"They looked captivated by each other," said an onlooker.

Meanwhile, a source close to Martin revealed: "She's had her eye on Jamie Johnson for a while. She thinks he's gorgeous, loves his new short haircut, and really hopes something can happen between them."

Looks like Johnson knows how to score off the pitch too!

And there in full colour beneath the headlines was *that* picture of him and Loretta in the hotel, with her kissing him on the cheek!

28
Gone

"Hooray!!!!" shouted the players as Jamie walked into the breakfast room. "Casanova!!!!!"

Jamie took one look at the restaurant tables, which were covered with about twenty copies of the picture of him and Loretta, and walked straight back out.

There was no point in putting it off any further.

"Where is she?" he demanded, marching into the hotel hairdresser's. He was seething. Not just at the lies that had been written about him, but also at the fact that Jack would have read the newspaper too. People would be asking *her* what it felt like to have been "substituted". She'd think he was trying to get back at her for the interview after the Nigeria game. It was all a complete disaster.

"Who are you after, love?" asked a cheerful podgy woman, who was washing a female customer's hair.

"Loretta," Jamie said, almost choking on her name. "I need to speak to her. What time does she start?"

"Oh, Loretta doesn't work here any more. If you want to speak to her now, you'll have to go through her agent."

"Agent?!" Jamie repeated. "You're kidding me! What does *she* need an agent for?"

He stomped out. This was absolutely ludicrous!

Should he call Jack and try to explain or just leave it and hope it all went away? Both options seemed like losing ones. He sat down on the bed and scratched the back of his head, hard.

Instinctively, he went to spin his ring on his bedside table… And then his body went freezing cold. His heart stopped and a leaping feeling of panic enveloped him.

He frantically ripped away the duvet and all the sheets. Nothing. He got on his knees to search on the floor under the bed. Not there either.

He ransacked all the clothes in his cupboard, forcing his hand into every pocket of every piece of clothing … but there was no sign of it.

He checked the bath, the shower and the bedside table, but it wasn't in any of those places either.

His forehead was wet with sweat and his throat had contracted to such an extent that no air could get in or out.

With a shaking hand and a faltering voice, he picked up the phone in his room and called down to the hotel reception.

"Hi ... it's Jamie Johnson in room 121," he said, trying to sound calm despite the torrent of sickness that was welling up within him. "Listen, have you, by any chance, had a ring handed in to you?... Gold, it's got an inscription... I don't know, this morning... No, if I knew that, then I wouldn't be calling you would I?! Sorry, it's just I *have* to get it back... Yes ... please check everywhere. If you find it, call me straightaway – it doesn't matter what time it is – just call me ... please."

Jamie put the phone back down and sat on his bed, trying to force himself to breathe.

He looked down at his hand. Without his ring, his finger looked pale, white, vulnerable. It looked disgusting.

Jamie clenched his hand into a fist and ordered it to crash into his chin. He actually punched himself, such was the level of his fury.

He didn't just want to hurt himself. He wanted to destroy himself. It was all he deserved.

That ring meant more to him than any possession in the world.

Why was it that he seemed to lose everything in life that he cared about?

(29)

Jack Attack

Friday 22 June – the day before
the final group game v Argentina

"There *is* no romance," said Jamie grumpily. "That girl asked for a photograph. That's it. The papers just made the rest up. I'd appreciate it if we could stick to the football, please."

Jamie was in a bad mood and he wasn't prepared to change it, even for this TV interview with Jack. Like everyone else in the squad, he was bored of waiting and bored of talking. The days between the matches had seemed like weeks.

The manager had tried to liven the evenings up with group activities, but his maverick striker had not made it easy. When Sir Brian had suggested a night out at the movies, Duncan Farrell, famous for his fits of boredom,

137

had shaken his head and said he wasn't interested. Then the next day, the boss arranged for them all to go out to an Italian restaurant, and Farrell had said that he fancied going to see a film instead!

The players were going stir-crazy. At times the Riverside Hotel felt like a five-star prison. Meanwhile, Jamie had suddenly been hit by the horrible thought that maybe one of his teammates had stolen his ring. Or one of the backroom staff. He'd tried snooping around in people's bags, but then he'd realized *he* was the one who would end up looking like the thief.

Though she was trying to be professional, Jamie could tell Jack was in a bad mood today too. Her nostrils were flaring when she spoke. That was always one of the giveaway signs with her. Jamie knew them all. In fact, there was nothing that either Jamie or Jack could hide from each other. They always knew what the other was thinking.

"Yes, let's look ahead to that crucial game against Argentina tomorrow," Jack said, refusing to make eye contact with Jamie. "How do you feel about lining up against Mattheus Bertorelli? It's not exactly a secret that you two have, to put it mildly, had your differences."

Jamie nodded. Jack knew better than anyone about what had really happened; how Jamie had overheard Bertorelli planning to fix a Hawkstone match – a discovery which had resulted in his own club teammate going to prison.

"Yeah, it'll be fine," said Jamie. "It's all water under the bridge."

"Are you sure about that? I mean, Bertorelli's nickname in Argentina is 'The Skilful Assassin'," warned Jack. "With your previous injuries, aren't you worried that—"

"I *said* it'll be fine," insisted Jamie, getting irritated now. "We'll shake hands before the game and it'll be done."

As the interview finished, neither Jamie nor Jack said goodbye. They both just took off their microphones and walked away.

They may not have used the words out loud, but they were both thinking the same thing: *You can go to hell.*

Match Day

Saturday 23 June Result from 3 p.m.

France 5	-	1 Nigeria
J Santini. 17. 38		Ouche. 20
C Cougier. 59		Yoku Sent Off. 28
M Ferrin 74. 85		

Current Standings
Before Final Group Match
Group D

Teams	Played	For	Against	Points
Argentina	2	5	1	6
France	3	8	7	3
Scotland	2	4	3	3
Nigeria	3	2	8	3

Final Group Fixture

Scotland v Argentina
St James' Park
KICK-OFF 8 p.m.

Scotland require a win or draw to reach the last 16

"Hand it over, then," said Tommy, with an even bigger smile than usual, stretching out his open palm to Jamie.

"What?" said Jamie. There were twenty-five minutes left until kick-off. His mind was set to match mode.

"Your granddad's ring. Don't you want me to look after it for you?"

Jamie looked at the floor. Tommy must have been the only person in the whole Scotland set-up that didn't know Jamie had lost it. How had he not heard? Jamie must have asked every player ten times if they'd seen it.

He was just about to ask Tommy if he had any idea where the ring might be when Sir Brian Robertson intervened.

"Can I have a quick word?" Robertson asked, putting his arm around Jamie and taking him to a corner of the dressing room for one of their little chats.

"Don't wind him up," Robertson said to Jamie in a soft but icily clear voice.

"Who? Tommy? I was just going to ask him if he'd seen my r—"

"Bertorelli, Jamie. I'm talking about Bertorelli. Don't wind him up. We both know that he's going to come looking for you today, but I don't want you to give him any excuses. And, if he does, you just let the referee handle it and don't get involved. OK? Just play your normal game. This is very important, Jamie. This guy is not like us – he doesn't play by the same rules. Do you understand what I'm saying?"

"Yes," replied Jamie.

And what was more, he knew Robertson was right.

㉛
Bring It!

10 minutes before kick-off

Jamie could sense the cameras zoom in on him as he stepped forwards. He did not smile or make eye contact; he simply reached out his hand.

But Bertorelli completely ignored the handshake and walked straight past Jamie, offering only a look of pure hatred.

His eyes seemed to be saying: "You sent me to prison. Now I'm going to put you through hell."

Fine, Jamie thought to himself. *That was your last chance. If that's the way you want to play it, that's the way we'll play it. You can bring it any time you want.*

Bertorelli may have been nicknamed the The Skilful Assassin, but Jamie was no mug. He knew how to look after himself.

*

Jamie was just stretching his hamstrings when he felt someone behind him flicking his ear really hard. He spun around quickly to find a familiar face standing next to him, right there on the touchline.

"All right?" the figure beamed. It was an eleven-year-old boy with stud earrings and tracks in his hair.

"Robbie!" said Jamie. "What are you doing here?"

"Deerrr! You doughnut! I'm the ball boy – remember! You're the one that sorted it out for me with the football people"

"Oh, yeah," said Jamie, still distracted by his encounter with Bertorelli.

"Don't worry about him either," said Robbie, following the line of Jamie's resentful stare. "I've got something up my sleeve for him!"

The floodlights were on. The turf was lush, wet and ready. The fans were in place and an air of expectancy filled the ground.

Jamie stood in the centre circle with Duncan Farrell. The unique, unmistakeable scent of the freshly watered pitch was carried to him on the warm evening breeze.

The stage was set. This was what the World Cup was all about. This was what football was all about.

The referee blew his whistle.

Final Group Game

Scotland v Argentina
St James' Park
KICK-OFF 8 p.m.

"And right from the first kick, we can see the urgency that Argentina are injecting into their game. Playing their innovative 3-3-1-3 system, designed to win the midfield battle, they clearly want to finish top of the group, meaning they would avoid the huge obstacle that Brazil would represent in the next round.

"The ball is out for a throw-in and Mattheus Bertorelli, leading from the front, charges over to take a quick one, but what's happening there? The ballboy seems to be holding on to the ball... Hang on ... is he juggling with it?"

Robbie Simmonds flicked the ball up into the air. He knew he was being cheeky and that he shouldn't be doing this but *What the hell?* he thought to himself. *I'm on camera, there are loads of people watching – this is my chance to show off my skills!*

Robbie balanced the ball carefully on his forehead before flicking the ball back into the air and then allowing it to land on his neck.

Now, some of the fans were beginning to take

notice, giving Robbie a little cheer or two. That was all the incentive he needed to carry on, so although he was now aware that Bertorelli was arrogantly waiting for the ball, Robbie just completely ignored him. Instead he dropped his body to the ground and did a set of five perfect press-ups, all with the ball balancing on his back!

"Nice one!" shouted the fans, now laughing and clapping as Robbie leapt back to his feet, giving one of the girls a wink as he began juggling the ball in time to their applause.

"Hey! Give the ball! Now!!" Bertorelli venomously shouted in Robbie's direction.

But Robbie was still having way too much fun to end the party here. He did a couple of around-the-worlds to make sure that everyone was aware of all of his street skills.

"Idiot!!" Bertorelli roared. "Give the ball or I kick you in face!"

But Robbie wasn't scared of Bertorelli. He'd grown up having scraps every day with his older brother, Dillon, who was much bigger and harder than Bertorelli.

You want your ball back? Robbie laughed to himself as Bertorelli now strode angrily towards him. *Fine, you can have it back!*

And with that, Robbie did a final back-heel into the

air before volleying the ball right at Bertorelli. In exactly the area where it hurt most!

Bertorelli slumped to the ground while Robbie turned to bow to the crowd. The Tartan Army loved him!

The referee, however, was not so amused and ran over to help Bertorelli. He immediately ordered Robbie to be sent away from the pitch.

But Robbie didn't seem the slightest bit concerned; he was accepting and even milking the standing ovation he was receiving from the fans as though he were a seasoned showbiz star! He even blew a couple of kisses into the crowd before disappearing down the tunnel.

Bertorelli pushed the referee away and quickly got back to his feet to take the throw, but Jamie could see that he was still hurt. He knew that a kick in the goolies was agony no matter how much you tried to hide it!

Obviously what Robbie had done was wrong, but somehow Jamie couldn't help but smile. Robbie was one of those people who just seemed to get away with breaking the rules. Besides, it had brought the crowd to life too. The Tartan Army were now in full voice with "Flower of Scotland". They had loved Robbie's little turn.

Not that Jamie was about to let Robbie take all the glory.

He was ready to turn up the heat on Argentina, and he knew exactly who he wanted to burn.

The moment Bertorelli next had the ball, Jamie left his station on the left wing and sped across the pitch to close down his opposite number. Bertorelli was a great player and an experienced international competitor, but his skills were his shooting, his set-pieces and his distribution – not his dribbling. Moreover, he was still recovering from Robbie's strike right in the bullseye!

Suddenly aware of the close attention he was receiving from Jamie, Bertorelli tried to wheel away, swinging his elbows out dangerously.

But there was no way Bertorelli was going to escape. Jamie avoided the elbow jabs and nipped in to steal the ball. As soon as he had it, he sprinted forwards with a blistering turn of pace.

Cutting inside on his left foot, he bore right through the heart of the Argentinian defence, which had no power to resist the charms of his charge.

Only a blatant shoulder barge from the rugged Argentinian centre-half, Juan Rattin, was able to stop Jamie when surely his second goal of the tournament awaited him.

"Johnson goes down … and is it? Yes it is! The referee had no hesitation. He's pointed to the spot. And Scotland have been awarded a penalty here! Even though the Argentinian players are surrounding the

*referee, they can't really have any complaints. Yes,
you can see it there on the replay – it's a stonewaller.
Definite spot-kick. And now, Johnson picks himself up
and dusts himself down. He's yet to miss a penalty in
professional football and he'll be hoping to keep that
record going now."*

Jamie loved taking penalties. He felt it was the mark of
a top player, a true talent, to be able to step up in any
circumstance and dispatch the ball home. Yes, it was
easy in a practice match or even in a league game when
you were already 2-0 up. But to take the responsibility
for a crucial spot-kick in a match as big as this? It was
Jamie's chance to prove to the world that he was born
to play this game.

He took a deep breath and kissed the ball. Then he
placed it down on the penalty spot and took two steps
back. His routine had been perfected over many years.
His technique honed by hundreds of hours of practice.
All to ensure that, when the moment came, he would
be able to do what he had been put on this earth to do.
That purpose was to stick the ball into the back of the
net and that moment was now. Right now.

Jamie sprinted hard at the ball to suggest he was
going to thump it low and hard into the corner of the
net but then – at the very last second – he slowed right

down and, as calm as you like, simply chipped the ball straight down the middle of the goal! He sent it sailing softly through the air like a dandelion seed, drifting lazily on the wind. The keeper was flummoxed, flailing but failing to save it. Goal!

"Now that is how to take a penalty! And so confident too! Looks like the ballboy is not the only cheeky one out there tonight! Johnson gives Scotland the lead in quite audacious style!"

Scotland 1   -   0 Argentina
J Johnson. 29 pen

On his way back to his own half, Jamie made sure he ran back past Bertorelli and, when he did so, he gave him a massive smile. He wasn't scared and he wanted Bertorelli to know it.

The rest of the half was punctuated with fouls and skirmishes, leaving precious little room for football, but that was fine with Scotland. A win would do them very nicely indeed. In fact, if they could get another goal, then they would top the group at Argentina's expense.

Scotland 1   -   0 Argentina
J Johnson. 29 pen
HALF-TIME

As Jamie headed down the tunnel, Bertorelli was already there, waiting for him, and as soon as Jamie got within five yards, the Argentinian began shouting.

It was a stream of verbal venom, each word a bullet of bitterness.

At first, Jamie wasn't too bothered. He remembered what Brian Robertson had said to him before the game about not getting involved, and anyway, he couldn't speak Spanish so he had no idea what Bertorelli was actually saying. He assumed Bertorelli was swearing but the only word he thought he could make out sounded like "poo". But that wasn't *too* bad anyway.

So, even in the face of Bertorelli's abuse, Jamie kept his cool.

"Is that all you've got, mate?" he smiled. "You know what? It's actually sad looking at you. I feel sorry for you, I really do. You're an embarrassment."

And then a look in Bertorelli's eyes made Jamie understand, perhaps for the first time, the level of hatred that the man had for him.

Perhaps it was at that moment that Jamie should have realized that whatever this thing was between him and Bertorelli – a war, a vendetta, perhaps even a curse – it was nowhere near over.

The flames of Bertorelli's anger burned in his dark, evil eyes as he coiled his neck back like a cobra.

And with that Bertorelli spat at Jamie. Right into his eye. Jamie could feel the slimy spit mingling with the moistness of the jelly in his eyeball. He closed his eye and felt some of the saliva slip down the side of his cheek.

Jamie just snapped. Instantly something inside him went off and he flew at Bertorelli with a rage that went beyond anything he had ever experienced before. It was as if some maniac had entered his body.

Jamie pulled back his fist. He wanted to slam it with all his might at Bertorelli's putrid face.

But, before he could take a swing, a bigger, more powerful hand intervened.

"You sure you want to do that, Jamie?" asked Cameron McManus, Scotland's warrior of a captain, whilst staring down Bertorelli. "It's exactly what he wants."

Jamie looked at his skipper. McManus didn't talk very often, so when he did, people tended to listen.

"You're right," said Jamie, starting to recover his composure. "I'd rather stick it to him on the pitch instead."

Scotland 1 - 0 Argentina
SECOND-HALF

The second half began again with Scotland immediately

recapturing the superiority they had achieved before half-time and now, the longer this game was going on, the more Jamie was growing in confidence.

Yes, he'd taken a couple of games to find his feet at international level, and it had been far from easy to win over the Tartan Army, but now, not only did they accept him as one of their own, he was swiftly becoming their favourite son.

At this moment, with thirty thousand fans singing his name, Jamie Johnson felt completely at home on the world stage: one Jamie Johnson, there's only one Jamie Johnson.

In fact, he now had the warm belief that maybe his granddad Mike had been right all those years: perhaps he *had* always been destined to play international football. This was where his talent belonged and now, as a long throw from Allie Stone sailed towards him, Jamie was ready to prove it once and for all.

Jamie instantly killed the pace on the ball, deftly cushioning it on his thigh. As it dropped to the ground, he flicked it forwards and glided after it in one easy, fluid movement.

Using his perfect close control, he passed the ball from foot to foot, nimbly evading the tackles like a speeding slalom skier racing down a mountain.

With his arms pumping and his legs racing, he

galloped down the line. Once he hit turbo speed, Jamie was simply uncatchable.

He was a superhuman playing against mortals. His skills came from another world.

A huge grin was plastered across his face as he teased and destroyed the defenders with his speed and poise. He could beat anyone today and he knew it.

However, what Jamie didn't know was that, chasing behind him, desperately trying to stay with him, was Mattheus Bertorelli.

All of Bertorelli's fury and bitterness had been brought to the boil and he was now charging after Jamie like an angry bull.

Perhaps, if Jamie had been able to see the savage, vengeful expression painted on Bertorelli's face, he might have been able to predict what was about to happen next.

Perhaps he might not have slowed down to bring out his step-overs to tease the last defender into a tackle.

The cruel finger of fate was about to point at Jamie and yet, with his eyes still firmly fixed on the ball, he had no idea at all...

"And Johnson now, rampaging through the Argentinian defence. They're not content with a 1-0 victory, they want a second! Still Johnson... He's past

three ... past four... And still Johnson goes on – just witness the pace! A step-over now, and another one! ... But look at Bertorelli! He's charging back at Johnson now and ... oh! Oh no! That is an awful tackle. He's hacked down Johnson from behind with a crushing foul. Oh, and the replay makes it look even worse! He's trapped Johnson's knee between his legs... Apologies to those watching at home who are squeamish... Those replays showing the knee being bent almost backwards are quite sickening..."

The stabbing pain shot through Jamie as he lay crumpled in a heap on the ground.

Writhing in agony, he raised his hand in the air to call for the physio. Almost instantly he felt a cold hand on his shoulder.

But when he opened his eyes, he did not see the physio or one of his teammates, he saw the smiling face of an assassin.

"Now you got what you deserve," said Bertorelli, leering over him. "I hope you never play again."

Bertorelli was instantly shown the red card by the referee, but a ten-year prison sentence would have been a more appropriate punishment.

Not that Bertorelli was going back behind bars or anywhere else. He stayed exactly where he was, standing over Jamie, laughing at him, while Jamie was lying prone on the ground, clutching his knee in agony.

Jamie almost couldn't see through the pain. The torture tore through him like a furious forest fire. Bertorelli had known exactly what he was doing. In an evil scissors motion, he'd wrapped himself around Jamie's knee, crushing it and twisting it until it almost broke.

Now, as Jamie was carefully lifted on to a stretcher and given oxygen to breathe in, the pain was almost too much to bear.

All that training ... all that practice ... all those hours fighting his way back from the last injury. It had all been about this; reaching the World Cup and showing the entire world his skill.

But now Bertorelli had killed those dreams. He'd slashed them apart in cruel, cold-blooded revenge.

Jamie covered his eyes as he was carried away from the pitch into the darkness of the tunnel. He couldn't believe that this was it. That it was all over.

32
GONE

"Don't touch it! Please!" Jamie shouted as the physio and the doctor laid him out on the treatment table in the dressing room and tried to examine his injury.

"Please!" he repeated, in agony. "Just leave me alone."

Jamie closed his eyes and felt the moisture of his tears trickle down his cheeks.

Meanwhile, back out on the pitch, insult was added to injury when, late in the game, the Argentina centre forward Madistuta connected powerfully with a volley at the far post to flash the ball past Allie Stone and into the back of the net.

FULL-TIME
Scotland 1   -   1 Argentina
J Johnson, 29 pen   G Madistuta, 81
                        M Bertorelli sent off, 72

Argentina celebrated the draw like a victory, with Bertorelli even running back on to the pitch to join in, pumping his fist backwards and forwards in joy, right in front of the Tartan Army.

The same player who had removed Scotland's star man with a diabolical tackle was now celebrating right in front of Scotland's fans, taunting them with his wolfish grin. He might as well have been trampling on their grave.

It was too much for Sir Brian Robertson. As various players began swapping shirts, he leapt from the dugout and began shouting at his own player, Pat Renton, who was, for some unknown reason, about to swap shirts with Bertorelli.

Robertson sprinted on to the pitch and pulled Renton's shirt back down on to his chest.

"Renton," he growled. "There's no way on earth that snake's having your shirt."

Group D – Final Standings

Teams	Played	For	Against	Points
Argentina	3	6	2	7
Scotland	3	5	4	4
France	3	8	7	3
Nigeria	3	2	8	3

Argentina and Scotland both through to the next round.

Scotland Progress

But is Johnson's Dream Wrecked?

Scotland have qualified from the so-called Group of Death to set up a mouth-watering second round clash with Brazil, but star player Jamie Johnson may have kicked his last ball at this World Cup. Having inspired Scotland again last night, he was cruelly cut down by a scything tackle from club teammate Mattheus Bertorelli.

IN BRIEF

COX UNFIT TO PL

"I was trying to help the kids" whined Cox at yesterday's pres conference.

"I was showing them the Rainb Kick, when my ankle just gave way It was agony but what made it worse was those horrible kids just laughed. That's the last tim ever help those brats." Twelve year old Adam Hopgood said ' always thought he was rubbish but he can't even step over a b without falling on his ar

Vital draw for Scotland – but at what cost?

The Scotland manager refused to answer questions on the tackle made by Bertorelli, saying only: "There should be a black card in football. For fouls worse than just a normal sending off. If I've ever seen a black card tackle, that was it."

Bertorelli Given Lengthy Ban

The Argentinian forward has been banned from three matches for his horror tackle on Jamie Johnson. But the Argentinian FA say they are to appeal against the decision, calling it an "overreaction".

OWN GOAL

attempted to slip behind the
ng disaster was almost averted
icked. Samuels claimed, once
divets all over the place. Spent

FOOTBALL

IN BRIEF

Winger set for hospital scans today

Johnson, who was carried from the field in tears, will discover this morning if he has any chance of playing again during the tournament, but sources close to the Scotland squad fear his World Cup may already be over.

Japan's Invasion

Three Japanese players are set to turn the game head

Time

Sunday 24 June

"Well, the ligaments aren't torn or ruptured; they are just very badly strained, so with some rest and regular physio, you should be ready for the start of the next season with Hawkstone."

"What?" blurted Jamie. "Next season? You're kidding me, doc! We're in the middle of the World Cup here – I need to play against Brazil!"

But the Scotland Team doctor was unmoved.

"Jamie, the fact that your knee has ballooned up to three times its normal size should tell you that you've got a pretty nasty injury," he said. "In fact, looking at the scans, your knee's actually in a worse state than I thought. It links back to the injury you sustained two years ago."

"The severe nature of the trauma you suffered in your car accident has meant that, ever since then, your body – all your ligaments and tendons – has been overcompensating to protect it and, as a result, every time you play, you are actually doing more damage to yourself. Your knee joint already has the wear and tear we might expect in a fifty-year-old."

The doctor drew in a deep breath and solemnly rubbed his jaw with his thumb.

"I'm very sorry to have to be the one to tell you this, Jamie, but even when you recover from this injury, your body is simply not in a position to carry this strain for much longer. I couldn't, in all honesty, see you playing professional football much beyond the age of twenty-five."

A silence wedged itself between them. The words just seemed to remain there, suspended in the air.

"But," said the doctor, suddenly aware that Jamie had not flinched or shown any kind of reaction during the entire time he had been talking, "you knew that already, didn't you?"

Jamie nodded. He didn't need a doctor to tell him that his body would not be able to play football at the top level for *very* much longer. He could feel it every day. Every time he twisted and turned, and every time he went in for a tackle. He'd fought his way back to fitness but he knew his knee would never be the same as it was before his injury. That was part of the reason that he played every single game as though it could be his last.

"Look, doc," said Jamie. "Forget about the future – just for a minute. Let's talk about now. Just give it to me straight. Is there any way you can get me back on that pitch for our next game?"

"No," answered the doctor, putting his equipment away. "The knee needs complete and utter rest in order to heal. There's no substitute for that. We're talking weeks, possibly a couple of months to build you back up. There's no way we could do it without seriously risking your health."

"Hang on a minute, doc. What are you saying? Does that mean it *is* possible or not? OK, let me put it another way. If your life depended on it, if there was no other choice, how would you get me on to that pitch to play against Brazil?"

"Round the clock physiotherapy, intense cryotherapy and an absurdly high number of painkilling injections," replied the doctor as though he were in an exam. "We might even be able to get you through the game itself, but the point is you'd be playing roulette with your career. I'd give you a fifteen per cent chance – at best – of getting away with it without doing some very serious long-term damage to yourself."

"Good," said Jamie, hobbling to his feet. "Well, I think I'll take my chances."

34

"Don't throw it away"

Monday 25 June

"I'm here to stop you," said Archie Fairclough, capturing Jamie's gaze and not letting it go. He'd come down from Hawkstone to the Scotland Team hotel and asked to see Jamie. In private.

"Stop me?"

"Yes, stop you. The doctor told me that you're considering playing on, so I'm here to stop you from making what could the biggest mistake of your life."

Jamie stared at Archie. "He told you about the fact that I might not have too much longer?"

Archie nodded. "You're our player, Jamie. Hawkstone pay your wages; we know everything about you...

Look, I realize how much you want to play at this World Cup – I get that. Of course I do. And I know that you hate being told what to do but, for once, you've got to listen. Come back to Hawkstone, Jamie. Let us treat you. Let us fix you like we did last time. It's the right thing to do."

"I can't, Archie. We're playing against Brazil! I just can't walk away from that. It's too big."

Archie let Jamie's words sink in. He put his finger over his lips and took in a long, deep breath.

"Well, then there's something else you need to know too, Jamie," he said, mysteriously.

"Yeah?" said Jamie, through furrowed eyebrows. "What?"

"Perhaps I shouldn't be showing you this now, but—"

"Come on, Archie, spit it out."

Archie didn't say anything. He simply picked a newspaper out of his bag and tossed it on to the table.

Jamie took one look at the paper and then stared blankly back at Archie; he didn't have a clue what any of the words on the page meant. They were written in another language.

El Barca intenta fichar al "Crack"

El juego del joven extremo escoces, Jamie Johnson, ha seducido al futbol club Barcelona. Este verano la directiva del club blaugrana tiene como su objetivo principal el fichaje del "Crack" y le hará una oferta astronómica al Hawkstone United para hacerse con sus servicios.

"It's true, Jamie," said Archie, softly. "They've come in for you."

"Who?" asked Jamie, feeling his chest begin to pound with excitement. There were only a couple of words he'd recognized in the whole article but they were enough for his mind to piece together an unbelievable puzzle. Jamie watched as his coach looked around the hotel lounge to check that no one was listening. Then Archie leaned forwards and said the name of Jamie's favourite club in the entire world.

"Barcelona."

Jamie was in shock.

"Are you serious?!" he shouted, standing up and grabbing the newspaper into his hands, trying to decipher its words. "They want me? I mean, I dreamed of it… Maybe one day … but I'm only eighteen! Oh my God, this is unbelievable!"

"Exactly," said Archie, calmly motioning for Jamie to sit back down. "They're utterly serious and they're talking very big money, huge money, the kind of money, well… Anyway, it's all the more reason why you need to think very carefully about risking everything over one game of football. Because, believe me, Barcelona won't touch you with a bargepole if they know you're playing on and doing irreparable damage with every kick of the ball."

Jamie felt the excitement slide away from him. It was as if he'd been given the best present he could possibly imagine, but somehow knew he couldn't accept it. It was a kind of tragic ecstasy.

"Yeah, well, what if, right now, my country's the most important thing to me, Archie?" he said, pushing the paper back across the table. "What if I said to you that right now I don't care about anything else?"

"Then I'd call you a liar. Even *you* know there are some things in life that are more important than football. This isn't just about the World Cup or even Barcelona, Jamie. It's about your *future*. And your family. Are you honestly telling me that, after all the injuries you've had, you now want to do *more* damage to yourself? Permanent damage? Because I don't believe that you do. Look at me, Jamie. Do you want your mum to grow old pushing you around in a wheelchair? You're always talking about your granddad and what a great player he 'could' have been. Well, do you want to end up like him? Or worse? Because – make no mistake – that's what we could be talking about here."

Jamie stared at the floor. That image was a dagger through his heart. He slumped into silence.

"No," he said. "No, I don't want that."

"I'm not trying to frighten you, Jamie," said Archie, tipping his head back to look at the ceiling as he searched for the right words. "It's just that – do you know how long people in football have been waiting for a player like you to come along? What you've got, Jamie … it's just too special; too special to throw away for *one* game. Please, Jamie – please, don't throw it away."

35
Packing Up

The phone rang in Jamie's room. He picked it up instantly, some warped part of his brain hoping it was Brian Robertson making a last-ditch attempt to convince Jamie to stay on, to play on through the pain barrier for him.

But he knew that would never happen. When Jamie had told Robertson and the rest of the squad that afternoon that he had to go back to Hawkstone "on doctor's orders", he'd been able to see the disappointment in his teammates' faces. They were visibly distressed and several of them had even told Jamie privately that they knew they had no chance against Brazil without him. But Sir Brian Robertson had been typically wise and supportive. He had put no pressure on Jamie to change his mind. "You know your body best, Jamie," he'd accepted, firmly shaking Jamie's hand. "So listen to what it's telling you."

"Your taxi's been ordered, sir," said the efficiently cold voice of the hotel receptionist. "It should be here in ten minutes."

"Right," replied Jamie. "I'll be down in a sec."

Jamie zipped up his suitcase and took a final look around his hotel room. Still no sign of the ring. He wondered if whoever had it knew how much pain they had caused to Jamie. No matter how much money they had sold it for, he would have given them double – anything they wanted – just to put it on his finger again. Just to feel close to Mike once more.

But the ring was gone and so too was Jamie's World Cup dream. True, he'd still only be twenty-two when the next World Cup came around, but what state would his body be in by then?

Jamie knew there was no way he could have argued with Archie. That vision of his mum pushing him around in a wheelchair was too haunting to ignore. Not to mention the fact that he'd be throwing away a potential move to Barcelona. If there was one club in the world that he was desperate to play for apart from Hawkstone, it was Barca.

So, for once in his life, he was going to listen to the

advice he was given. Take the sensible option. Follow his head and not his heart.

He took one last look around his room. The World Cup wall chart was only half complete. And that was how it would remain.

Final Group A Table

Team	P	W	D	L	F	A	GD	Pts
Portugal	3	2	1	0	4	1	3	7
Chile	3	1	1	1	3	2	1	4
South Africa	3	1	1	1	4	5	-1	4
Morocco	3	0	1	2	1	4	-3	1

Group A Results

Date	Fixture		
11th Jun	Sth Africa 1	-	1 Chile
11th Jun	Portugal 0	-	0 Morocco
16th Jun	Sth Africa 1	-	3 Portugal
17th Jun	Morocco 1	-	2 Chile
22nd Jun	Chile 0	-	1 Portugal
22nd Jun	Morocco 1	-	2 Sth Africa

Final Group B Table

Team	P	W	D	L	F	A	GD	Pts
Germany	3	3	0	0	7	1	6	9
Sth Korea	3	1	1	1	5	6	-1	4
Greece	3	1	0	2	2	5	-3	3
Australia	3	0	1	2	3	5	-2	1

Group B Results

Date	Fixture		
11th Jun	Sth Korea 2	-	0 Greece
12th Jun	Germany 1	-	0 Australia
16th Jun	Germany 4	-	1 Sth Korea
17th Jun	Greece 2	-	1 Australia
22nd Jun	Australia 2	-	2 Sth Korea
22nd Jun	Greece 0	-	2 Germany

Final Group C Table

Team	P	W	D	L	F	A	GD	Pts
Brazil	3	1	2	0	4	3	1	7
Russia	3	1	2	0	2	1	1	4
USA	3	1	1	1	3	3	0	4
Iraq	3	0	1	2	0	2	-2	1

Group C Results

Date	Fixture
12th Jun	Russia 1 - 1 Brazil
13th Jun	Iraq 0 - 1 USA
18th Jun	USA 2 - 2 Brazil
18th Jun	Russia 0 - 0 Iraq
23rd Jun	USA 0 - 1 Russia
23rd Jun	Brazil 1 - 0 Iraq

Final Group D Table

Team	P	W	D	L	F	A	GD	Pts
Argentina	3	2	1	0	6	2	4	7
Scotland	3	1	1	1	5	4	1	4
France	3	1	0	2	8	7	1	3
Nigeria	3	1	0	2	2	8	-6	3

Group D Results

Date	Fixture
13th Jun	Scotland 0 - 1 Nigeria
13th Jun	Argentina 2 - 1 France
18th Jun	France 2 - 4 Scotland
18th Jun	Nigeria 0 - 3 Argentina
23rd Jun	France 5 - 1 Nigeria
23rd Jun	Scotland 1 - 1 Argentina

Final Group E Table

Team	P	W	D	L	F	A	GD	Pts
Spain	3	3	0	0	5	1	4	9
Ivory Coast	3	2	0	1	4	2	2	6
Canada	3	1	0	2	3	6	−3	3
Denmark	3	0	0	3	2	5	−3	0

Group E Results

Date	Fixture
14th Jun	Spain 2 – 0 Canada
14th Jun	Ivory Coast 1 – 0 Denmark
19th Jun	Spain 1 – 0 Ivory Coast
19th Jun	Denmark 1 – 2 Canada
24th Jun	Canada 1 – 3 Ivory Coast
24th Jun	Denmark 1 – 2 Spain

Final Group F Table

Team	P	W	D	L	F	A	GD	Pts
Turkey	3	1	2	0	3	1	2	5
England	3	1	1	1	4	5	−1	4
Belgium	3	0	3	0	2	2	0	3
Egypt	3	0	2	1	4	5	−1	2

Group F Results

Date	Fixture
14th Jun	Egypt 1 – 1 Turkey
15th Jun	Belgium 1 – 1 England
20th Jun	England 0 – 2 Turkey
20th Jun	Egypt 1 – 1 Belgium
24th Jun	England 3 – 2 Egypt
24th Jun	Turkey 0 – 0 Belgium

Final Group G Table

Team	P	W	D	L	F	A	GD	Pts
Italy	3	2	1	0	5	2	3	7
Japan	3	1	2	0	7	0	7	5
Honduras	3	1	1	1	4	3	1	4
Switzerland	3	0	0	3	1	12	−11	0

	Date	Fixture
Group G Results	15th Jun	Honduras 0 - 0 Japan
	15th Jun	Italy 2 - 1 Switzerland
	20th Jun	Italy 3 - 1 Honduras
	21st Jun	Japan 7 - 0 Switzerland
	25th Jun	Switzerland 0 - 3 Honduras
	25th Jun	Japan 0 - 0 Italy

Final Group H Table

Team	P	W	D	L	F	A	GD	Pts
Holland	3	2	0	1	4	2	2	6
Norway	3	2	0	1	3	2	1	6
Cameroon	3	1	1	1	1	1	0	4
Croatia	3	0	1	2	0	3	−3	1

	Date	Fixture
Group H Results	16th Jun	Croatia 0 - 1 Norway
	16th Jun	Holland 0 - 1 Cameroon
	21st Jun	Norway 1 - 0 Cameroon
	21st Jun	Holland 2 - 0 Croatia
	25th Jun	Cameroon 0 - 0 Croatia
	25th Jun	Norway 1 - 2 Holland

SECOND ROUND FIXTURES
Portugal v South Korea
Brazil v Scotland
Argentina v Russia
Germany v Chile
Spain v Italy
England v Norway
Turkey v Ivory Coast
Holland v Japan

So this was it. Three games, two goals and one Man of the Match award…

Not bad, Jamie thought to himself. *At least I can always say I've played in the World Cup. No one can ever take that away from me.*

Jamie knocked on the door of the manager's office. His taxi would be here soon but he had one last person to say goodbye to first.

There was no answer, so Jamie opened the door to find that only Tommy the kit man was in there, putting all his effort into shining up Sir Brian's boots.

"All right, Tom? Where's the gaffer?" asked Jamie. "I need to say goodbye."

Jamie wished he could have had more games under Sir Brian. He respected him so much. For his honesty, for his belief in his players and for the way he'd always stood up for Jamie – even when other people had doubted him. It made Jamie's stomach lurch with regret to think that he'd now be leaving Robertson and the rest of the squad to carry on the fight without him.

Without interrupting his polishing, Tommy simply pointed a remote control at the TV screen and turned it up.

Sir Brian was in the press tent, which was over on the other side of the hotel grounds, giving a press conference, which was being televised live.

"I mean, it was always going to be an uphill struggle for Scotland and now, if the rumours are to be believed, your best player has just told his teammates he's out of the World Cup. Johnson is the one that has taken this team to the next level so, without him, how do you plan to take on and beat a football superpower like Brazil, Sir Brian?"

Brian Robertson smiled and took the question in his stride.

"This World Cup has thrown up some unpredictable results, though, hasn't it?" he purred. "Who would have thought that Japan would have beaten Switzerland seven nil? Look at how well Turkey and Norway have both done. Who knows? England might even win a penalty shoot-out!"

While the press room enjoyed Robertson's humour, he carried on.

"My point is, football doesn't always go the way you think it's going to – there's always a twist around the corner. Yes, Brazil are a fantastic side with some exceptional players, but in my humble opinion they haven't been quite at their best so far this tournament… And anyway, you know what? Sometimes, it's just more fun being David rather than Goliath. There's no pressure on us to beat Brazil, so we can just go out there and enjoy it."

"OK, Sir Brian, on another subject, I don't know if you've heard this yet – but it's being reported by the Argentinian press that Mattheus Bertorelli has just had his suspension reduced from three matches to one match on appeal. Do you have any comment on that?"

"You're joking, aren't you?" growled Robertson, immediately losing the smile from his face.

"No. It's just been confirmed. A statement has gone up on the website."

"You want my comment? You want to know what I think?" said Robertson, slamming his fist down hard on to the table. "Disgrace. That's what it is. An absolute disgrace. That tackle he made on Jamie Johnson was barbaric. He was a snake in the grass; he'd been waiting all game for his opportunity to attack Johnson. And then he did it. So now my player's out of the entire tournament and that animal misses one match. *One* match! How's that fair? Where's the justice in that? The people who made that decision should hang their heads in shame. That's what I think."

"Do you not think you're going a little bit over the top about the tackle, Sir Brian? Those kind of words can get you in trouble."

"Not in the slightest. What he did wasn't a tackle. It was a violent assault. If the authorities can't see that, then they know even less about the game than I thought."

Jamie could not believe what he was hearing.

"Why's he saying all this, Tommy?" asked Jamie. "He's slaughtering them. They'll definitely ban him for this."

"Aye," smiled Tommy, continuing to scrub away at the boots. "They probably will and all but I guess sometimes you've just got to do what you believe in – otherwise, what's the point?"

"Yeah," said Jamie, subconsciously rubbing his finger in the spot where his ring should have been. It occurred to him that Tommy might be more right than he could ever know.

At that moment, there was a brisk knock at the door.

"Someone order a taxi up to Hawkstone?" asked a burly man, jangling a set of keys in his hand.

"Yeah, that's me," said Jamie, walking slowly and regretfully towards him.

So, this was it. The end of the road. The final whistle—

"But listen, mate, I'd better give you a big tip because I'm going to need to cancel that cab," smiled Jamie.

"Really?" asked both the cab driver and a stunned Tommy, who had even paused in his polishing to look up at Jamie.

"Yeah," Jamie nodded, immediately feeling the weight of a thousand future regrets lift from his shoulders. "I'm not ready to leave yet. I'm not going anywhere."

36

History Repeating

Tuesday 26 June – one day before second round match Scotland v Brazil

"Don't be silly, Mum!" said Jamie. "We trained today and I was absolutely fine!"

"Well, all I know is what happened with Dad," said Jamie's mum. She was calling from the cruise that Jeremy had booked for her birthday. Who would want to go on a cruise while the World Cup was being held in your own country?! It always amazed Jamie how he could live with two people who had such little interest in football! Still, it was reassuring for Jamie to hear her voice because it reminded him that life still went on outside of all the hysteria surrounding the World Cup.

"After his injury, Dad tried to play on when the doctors told him not to – that's how he ended up with his arthritis. You know what he was like, Jamie. He could hardly walk when he got older and I'm sure that's why his heart…"

Jamie's mum didn't finish her sentence. Her voice just trailed off as it always did when she talked about Mike and what happened. Even though it was a couple of years ago now, it still haunted them both… Those horrible, unanswerable questions about whether there was anything they could have done to prevent it. Certainly, Jamie's mum, who was a nurse at the local hospital, had her own theories about why Mike's heart had given out.

"Look," said Jamie, trying to find some brightness to balance out the sadness he could hear on the other end of the line. "I understand what you're saying, but just because that happened to Mike doesn't mean it has to happen to me. Mike's injury was yonks ago. Things have changed completely. They have different ways of dealing with injuries now. You know that. I mean, you should see this freezing ice chamber they've put me in. It's amazing. It gets the blood flowing more quickly to make me heal faster. Actually – no, I've just realized you wouldn't like it, Mum; way too cold for you!"

There was a pause. Jamie was glad he'd left out the

fact that he'd been getting daily painkilling injections too. Although his mum dealt with gory stuff all the time at hospital, she was still extra sensitive whenever anything happened to Jamie.

"Just make sure my boy comes back to me in one piece," she said finally.

"I will," Jamie smiled. "And remember, if we're losing against Brazil, can you make sure you go to the toilet, please? You know that's the only sure-fire way to guarantee me scoring a goal!"

37

Status Update

That night

Jamie used his new mobile to log on to the net. He was so happy to have a phone again – being without one for these few days had felt as if he was missing an arm. But now it had arrived, it seemed as though the wait had been worth it – the apps were fantastic and the internet speed unbelievable.

Besides, there was not a lot else for Jamie to do. He'd already listened to all his music and watched South Korea knock out Portugal in a stunning second-round match, which had instantly been called one of the games of the tournament.

Apart from training and meals, the only other time

he'd even been out of his room today was for the four o'clock team meeting in which Sir Brian Robertson had confirmed to the squad that, following his press conference outburst, he had been banned from the match against Brazil. Completely. He was not to sit in the dugout, go into the dressing room or have any kind of contact with his players during the match.

It was a massive blow but Robertson had played it down.

"You'll be fine," he'd said. "I've drummed everything into you so much that you'll know what I would have said anyway! Just make sure you all get a good night's sleep this evening. That's as important as anything else."

But Jamie knew he wouldn't be able to get to sleep for hours yet. That was why he was surfing the net.

Once he'd checked the football gossip, he immediately did the one thing he shouldn't have done. He went straight to Jack's blog.

He knew it! She'd updated her home page with a really hot new photo. He wondered whether she'd done it just to annoy him because she thought he was with Loretta Martin now. She must have been angry with him because she hadn't even called to see if he was all right after his injury.

*

Jack's **FOOTBALL**

OMG! Having amazing time working at the World Cup! Learning every day and interviewing some of the best players in the world! Amazing! Come on, England – you can beat Norway and get into the Quarters!!

Jamie felt sick. They hadn't spoken for days and yet she still seemed like the happiest person on earth. She obviously wasn't missing him at all.

Right! Jamie thought to himself. *I'm going to accept all the friendship requests that I've got from any girls! I'll even accept one from Loretta Martin if it's there.* But when he went on to his own website there were none. Typical!

The only message in his inbox was from Robbie Simmonds.

Yo! Jamie J! Good to see the knee's OK and fanks for ballboy favour. The people in football want 2 ban me from being a ballboy ever again but I dont give a monkeys and they are LOSERS coz I'm already a star! Som1s put my juggling and kicking the ball at Berti on youtube and its had like THOUSANDS of hits! How cool is that?! I'm a STAR all over the WORLD!!!! OK, last favour – can you get me Rodinaldo's shirt after the Brazil game? Go on!!! Will be your best friend!!!

Laters, RTBFITW (Robbie The Best Footballer In The World!! ... OK maybe 2nd best after Rodinaldo!)

PS – Dillon is well jealous. He says Loretta Martin is FIIIIIIIIIIIIIIIIIIIIIIT! He wants 2 know how much you paid her to go out with you! 😔

Hey Rob – sorted ballboy for you. Michelle from English FA will be in touch... Be nice to her! BTW what's all this peace & love business?! U sum kind of hippy now?!

Jamie scrolled straight back to Jack's page. How did she manage to look so fine in every single photo? She looked way better than the models in magazines because her smile was real and she'd had none of that plastic surgery.

What was she doing now? While Jamie was stuck here, pacing the floor of his hotel room prison, she was probably out somewhere partying—

There was a loud knock on the door. So loud and powerful, in fact, that Jamie was not altogether surprised to see the huge figure of Duncan Farrell standing there when he opened it.

38
Popping Out

"All right!" said Duncan Farrell, smiling in the hallway outside Jamie's door. He was so tall he had to duck slightly to keep his head below the ceiling.

Jamie recognized this smile. It was Farrell's mischievous one. The same one he'd had at dinner last night, just before he'd slipped a fake cockroach into Allie Stone's bean soup.

"All right," offered Jamie, a little warily, wondering what exactly Farrell was up to.

"Fancy popping out?" Farrell enquired from behind his ever-widening grin.

Jamie had heard about this. Faz – as the team called him – was notorious for getting bored, so it was not unusual, especially in the run-up to a big game, for him to try to recruit a teammate for a little adventure as a way of breaking up the monotony of endless days in the hotel.

"Popping out? Like where?" Jamie asked. He was intrigued. Farrell was a loose cannon and Jamie couldn't help being drawn to people like that. One of the best stories he'd heard so far about Farrell was the time he'd excused himself from a team meeting before a big League game in Scotland, saying he needed to go to the toilet. He was then found seven days later, sitting in a bed in a hotel room in Paris, nonchalantly playing a guitar. The story had made Jamie laugh so much, and the best part was that Farrell couldn't even play the guitar!

"Reckon we should take a trip down to the river. Get out of this hotel."

The River Thames was easily accessible from the bottom of the hotel's gardens and Jamie could see it clearly from his room. Sometimes just knowing it was there had soothed Jamie when his mind had become blocked by the hugeness of what was going on around him. Every TV channel, every radio station and every newspaper was wall-to-wall with the World Cup. It seemed as if it was the only event happening on earth. So, just taking a minute to watch the water twisting and meandering, as it had for centuries on its inevitable passage to the sea, reminded Jamie that some things would continue long after this

World Cup was a distant memory.

"Erm," said Jamie, taking a sneaky look at his watch. 10.20 p.m. He also recalled the fact that Farrell's little adventures generally ended up in unmitigated disaster. "Yup, definitely. Let's go down to the river tomorrow. A walk before lunch sounds good—"

"Forget tomorrow," said Farrell, verbally cornering Jamie. "I'm talking about now. Come on, what are you scared of?"

"I'm not scared of anything. It's just we're playing against Brazil tomor—"

"Right then," said Farrell. "Meet you outside the fire exit in five minutes."

"Well, to be fair to you, Faz, that was actually a pretty good idea," said Jamie as they arrived back at the little jetty just below the hotel gardens. "You were right, we needed to escape from the prison for a bit."

They had walked for about twenty minutes, and although they hadn't talked much – Faz was more of a doer than a thinker – stretching his legs on a warm summer night had done Jamie a world of good. He would have only been stuck up in his room by himself otherwise.

"See you in the morning," said Jamie heading back up to the hotel.

"Oh, we ain't done yet," replied Farrell, who, by the

time Jamie had turned around, had already undone the ropes which attached a tiny rowing boat to the jetty.

"Hop in," said Farrell, as he jumped in and took a hold of the oars. "We'll row across to town. See if there's any life over there."

Jamie didn't move. He could see the bright lights, shining like distant stars on the other side of the river, but he wasn't the greatest of sailors and it was already getting pretty late.

"Or shall I tell the rest of the squad that you're a p—"

"OK! I'm coming!" said Jamie, leaping down into the little boat, which rocked from side to side in the water as it took account of the weighty presence of the two international footballers which it now carried. "I suppose this is one way to take your mind off the game."

It didn't take Jamie or Farrell very much time at all to work out that they were never going to make it to the other side.

Almost as soon as they pushed themselves away from the jetty, the current took hold of them. The oars were irrelevant as the power of the water dictated their speed and direction. While Farrell seemed to enjoy the danger of the situation, as though he were on some extreme fairground ride, Jamie honestly feared for his life as the tiny vessel flew downriver. The night was pitch-black. What if a big boat was coming the other way? They would never see Jamie and Faz in time. What if they smashed into a bridge? He could tell from the speed with which they were passing riverside cottages that they were travelling seriously fast. And they were out of control too. It was like being in a speeding car without any brakes.

Finally, after about five minutes, Farrell's face turned as pale as Jamie's. By now he had stopped laughing. If they carried on like this, they would end up somewhere near Southend – if they even made it that far alive.

"Right," said Farrell, standing up in the tiny boat, which by now was starting to leak freezing cold water. "This is my stop."

"What do you mean?" asked a panicked Jamie, only to see his teammate dive off the boat and attempt to swim to the riverbank.

Jamie quickly calculated the other options in his mind and realized immediately that there were none.

"Oh for God's sake," he shouted as he followed Farrell, plunging head-first into the cold and powerful current of the River Thames.

39
Dressing Down

Wearing a very strange combination of striped nightclothes that made them look somewhat older than they were, Scotland's World Cup stars, Jamie Johnson and Duncan Farrell finally got back to the Riverside Hotel just before 1.30 in the morning.

After initially trying to swim against the current, they had worked out that there was no point in fighting it, instead they allowed the river to carry them to where it wanted. Finally, on one of the bends, they had managed to catch hold of a low-hanging branch from a tree and haul themselves up on to the bank.

Not knowing where they were or how they were going to get back, they had resolved to try and enlist help.

As luck would have it, a kindly-looking old man had opened the first door they had knocked on.

Seeing the two shivering, soaking-wet young men standing on his doorstep, the man had taken pity on them and immediately invited them in and offered assistance.

"I'm afraid all I've got is some of my old pyjamas, but they're nice and warm," said the man, chuckling to himself as he came down the stairs with some fresh clothes for the pair. "You know, I've just realized who you two remind me of... You look like Jamie Johnson and you look like that nutter who plays up front for Scotland. Now what's his name? Duncan … Duncan…"

It was only when Faz had tilted his head and said the word "Farrell" that it had finally dawned on the genial old man exactly who was standing in his house at midnight on the night before Scotland were due to face Brazil.

Perhaps understandably, the man had almost fainted on the spot, but after a hot mug of tea had helped him regain his composure, he had been kind enough to call his local minicab firm to come and pick up the two wayward stars.

The driver had been so excited to have Johnson and Farrell in the back of his cab that he'd told them not to worry about the fact that they didn't have any money and, in exchange for a few autographs for his kids, he'd promised that he wouldn't breathe a word of it to the press.

It had actually looked as if they might get away with the whole escapade as the pair – modelling some very dodgy-looking striped pyjamas – tiptoed their way back into the hotel reception in the early hours of the morning.

However, right there waiting for them, wearing a look of pure rage, was Sir Brian Robertson.

Like two timid children facing an angry father, the players offered their best expressions of meek regret.

Robertson gave them both a look of utter contempt and said simply: "I'll deal with you two after the game."

Match Day

Wednesday 27 June – last 16 Match

Scotland v Brazil
White Hart Lane
KICK-OFF 8 p.m.

"OK," said the doctor. "You might feel a slight scratch."

Jamie tried not to look. He hated needles. The thought of the sharp metal piercing through the layers of his skin made him shiver … but he had no choice. If he wanted to play in this game, he needed to have this injection in his knee. The recurring memory of Mike's career ending at the age of seventeen, through injury, kept haunting him, but he told the evil whisper in his head to shut up.

This was the World Cup. This was *his* World Cup and nothing was going to stop him from playing.

"OK, all done," said the doctor, taking off his gloves. "You're getting used to these now, aren't you?"

"Yeah," said Jamie. He knew that was nothing to be proud of. What he was doing to his body was at best unnatural and at worst highly dangerous.

He stretched his knee backwards and forwards. Suddenly, he was completely pain free. He blocked the damage he was doing from his mind and focused on the only fact that mattered: he was going to be playing today.

It felt strange not to have the boss there with them in the dressing room. Everyone had expected him to be banned from the dugout. But not letting him even talk to his players in the dressing room seemed way too harsh. The room seemed so empty without his giant presence.

There were still forty minutes until kick-off and, without a pre-match team talk from the boss, Jamie went out on to the pristine pitch to warm up and take in the atmosphere. White Hart Lane was just starting to fill up. He looked up at the big TV screens that were housed high above the pitch.

They were broadcasting the press conference of Mario Caesar, Brazil's manager, from the day before. Jamie had watched it at the time so he knew what was coming next.

"Are you surprised that Jamie Johnson seems set to play – after what happened to him against Argentina?" the Scottish journalist had asked Caesar.

"With great players, nothing should surprise you," Caesar, an old, grey-haired legend of the game, had responded. "We know Jamie Johnson very well. We have watched many games of him. We know this player has a heart like a lion. In Brazil, we would call him *Fenomeno*. We will need to watch him very closely."

Jamie juggled the ball and pinged it into the back of the net. It was a perfect strike – one of those Jamie knew he'd nailed, almost before he had made contact with the ball. His body shape had been virtually immaculate.

A group of fans behind the goal instantly clapped and started cheering his name.

Jamie waved to them and nodded to a ballboy to chuck him another ball. *Fenomeno.* He'd look that one up after the game.

Jamie knew he and his teammates were going to be up against something special as soon as he saw the Brazil team come out to warm up.

While the Scotland players were diligently going through their short sprint exercises and keep-ball games, the Brazilians were intent on displaying their full array of tricks. Two of their players were even volleying the ball to each other from about twenty-five yards away. They kept smashing the ball at each other, first time, on the volley, without even letting the ball bounce. Jamie wondered if anyone in the crowd knew how hard that actually was to do. If he was honest, he would probably have paid just to watch them warm up!

Then Jamie zeroed in on Rodinaldo, the Brazilian playmaker and the current World Player of the Year. The number 10 had tilted his head back and was balancing the ball on his lips!

Jamie stared at him. His physique was immense. Most pacey attackers were short and fast like Jamie, using their skill, feints and swift changes of direction to manipulate the ball and shimmy past opponents. But this guy could do all of that as well as being six foot two inches tall and built like a cruiserweight boxer. He'd been timed doing the hundred metres in 10.54 seconds. In his football boots.

Jamie remembered that Robbie had asked him to get Rodinaldo's shirt after the game. *That would be fine,* Jamie thought to himself. *Only problem is, I've got to catch him first.*

(41)

Like Watching Brazil

Last 16 Match

If Jamie had thought Brazil were going to be the best team he'd ever played against, he was wrong. They were better than that.

They were the best team he had ever seen in his life and they seemed intent on giving Scotland the mother of all footballing lessons.

If any other team had teased and taunted Scotland the way that Brazil were doing now, Jamie would have assumed that they were taking the mickey on purpose. But these guys weren't. They were just having fun with a football.

Every time they tackled a Scotland player, they winked to one of their teammates, and each time one of their own moves broke down, they still indulged in a warm hug as soon as the ball went out of play.

They had so much time on the ball that, as they were spraying it around the pitch like a bunch of mates playing Frisbee in the park, they even raised their hands to thank their teammates for the pass, while the ball was still in the air on its way to them.

This was football on another level. From a different dimension.

Despite the fact that it had gone 8 p.m., the temperatures were unusually high, with a dry, static heat – which made it difficult to breathe – filling the windless air.

Chasing around the pitch after the ball like dogs being teased by cruel owners, the Scotland players visibly wilted in the extreme conditions. Even the contest between the fans was becoming one-sided. Despite the fact that the Tartan Army, with England being right on their doorstep, outnumbered the Brazilians by about five to one in the stadium, the colour and the noise being produced by the South Americans was unbelievable. The whistles, the Samba beats … the Brazilian girls! Watching the fans was almost as entertaining as watching the football.

But in truth, there was only one star attraction. Rodinaldo was running the show. His skills were sublime. He'd mastered the art of looking in one direction and passing in the other, and the speed of his feet on the ball was almost balletic.

His crowning moment had come ten minutes before half-time when he'd bent home a free-kick with such finesse and wizardry that Allie Stone had whacked his head on his own post as he attempted – in vain – to keep it out.

Jamie had watched on as Rodinaldo, with his trademark smile, had jogged casually over to the corner flag and, taking it gracefully into his hand, had proceeded to lead it in a little samba dance.

Jamie shook his head in admiration. Even the guy's celebrations were class.

Scotland 0 - 1 Brazil
                    Rodinaldo, 36
HALF-TIME

As they slipped feebly into the dressing room and collapsed on to the benches, every single one of the Scotland players was bathed in sweat. Panting and out of breath, they were still only halfway through the harshest lesson that football had ever taught them. Had it not been for a couple of quite stunning reflex saves from Allie Stone, Brazil would already have been out of sight.

What the Scotland players would have given to have had Sir Brian Robertson there with them. Now, more than ever before, they needed their manager.

And then, as if by a footballing miracle, the man himself suddenly appeared right in front of them.

His players were overcome by surprise and happiness.

"Boss!" they yelled. "What are you doing here? You're banned! What if they see y—"

"Never mind all that," snapped Robertson. "Now, do you want to get back into this game or not?"

42

World Class

There was hardly any time, but those few seconds were enough for Sir Brian Robertson to deliver the immortal lines to his team…

"World class," he said, stalking the dressing room, looking each of his players in the eye.

"Do you want to know what that means? What it *really* stands for? It means that, in the biggest game of your entire life, you look inside yourself and you find another level. You scale new heights and play better than you've ever done before."

Robertson let his words sink in. Then he smiled and continued in a hushed tone that made every one of his players listen ever more intently.

"Remember that old saying in football, boys – 'Form

is temporary and class is permanent.' That's true. But let me also tell you that world class – genuine world class – well, that's for ever.

"Are *you* world class? We're about to find out."

Scotland 0   -   1 Brazil
                 Rodinaldo, 36
SECOND-HALF

The referee checked with his linesman before bringing the whistle to his mouth to get the second half under way.

And then, almost at that exact moment, something happened which no one in the ground was expecting. Not even the experts had predicted it. But it was to change the entire course of the match and, for that matter, the World Cup. A cluster of thick black clouds suddenly covered the sky and there was a loud crack of thunder. For a moment, the night was eerily still. And then the heavens truly opened. The rain didn't just fall from the sky, it rushed down with tropical force. In just a few minutes, the entire pitch was drenched and all the players were so wet they looked as though they had been put in the washing machine by mistake.

For the second time in less than twenty-four hours, Jamie wondered whether he might actually drown.

But although the rain was pouring like a river from

his head and into his eyes, the water was also stirring something within him. It was sometimes in these conditions, when everything seemed to be going wrong, that Jamie found an extra, inner strength. Scotland were losing, they were heading out of the World Cup and the torrential rain was battering him and every other player on the pitch. It was time to give up.

Or stand up.

Jamie raced after Rodinaldo, who was making a dazzling dribble towards the Scotland goal. Rodinaldo was very, very quick, but Jamie at his top turbo speed was even faster. He pursued the Brazilian maestro and, when he was close enough, he launched himself into a sliding tackle.

Jamie slid across the slick, greasy turf, forcing the ball out of play, taking Rodinaldo with him as they both crashed into the hoarding boards.

Rodinaldo lay there, surprised and shaken by the force of the tackle. But Jamie was straight up, ready for the next challenge. He was smiling. He hadn't done a slide tackle like that – a proper one, skidding for yards – for years. Probably since he was at school, where it had been one of his trademarks.

The Tartan Army rose to their feet, encouraged by Jamie's show of heart and bravery. For the first time, they began to out-sing the soaking Brazilian fans. In fact, what was happening on the terraces was also a reflection of what was happening on the pitch. For as Jamie looked around him, he noticed that some of the Brazilian heads had begun to drop. They began slipping in the slick turf, looking suspiciously at their boots each time they lost their footing.

Soon – as their passes began to skid wildly off the grass and miss their targets – they could be seen staring at one another, at first quizzically, and then accusingly.

Their smiles had been replaced by frowns... They didn't like this.

Jamie was not normally one to shout loudly on the pitch, but this time he knew he had to. He could see what was going on and had to convey the message to his teammates.

This was their chance.

As another wayward Brazilian pass skipped out for a throw, he clapped his hands together so loudly it almost sounded as if a firecracker had been let off.

"Boys! Let's step it up now!" he roared through the sheets of pounding rain. "Look at them – they're there for the taking!"

Like a starter's gun setting off a sprint, Jamie's words were the signal for Scotland's players to step forwards; they were ready to make their move. Every member of the team ran for his teammate, every player covered, tracked, tackled and supported. And as soon as Brazil were in possession, Scotland swarmed around them like hungry wasps.

He may not have been there in the dugout, but Brian Robertson's team could still sense his presence and belief. They knew they were doing exactly what Robertson wanted. This was what playing as a team truly meant.

Soon, the pressure on Brazil began to tell. First, they resorted to hoofing long, aimless balls forwards, which only played into the hands of Scotland's brave giants at the back. Cameron McManus and Owen Tulley won every single header, bullying the Brazilian strikers into submission.

Then, when they realized that the long balls were never going to work, the Brazilians gave up on the idea of passing altogether. Instead, their flair players began to uncharacteristically hoard possession, lingering on the ball far too long, trying to do everything by themselves.

This was perfect for Jamie as, just after the hour, it allowed him to nip in and steal possession away from their central midfielders – snatching the ball like a cheeky pickpocket. He zoomed forward with a burst of electric speed, accelerating with each surging stride.

Facing up to the wall of defenders which converged on him, Jamie then shaped to pass, fooling the opposition so comprehensively that, just for a second, the defence seemed to open up and invite him through. It was as though he'd used a secret password to reveal a hidden gateway through the Brazil backline.

Jamie dashed through the gap and into the box, the ball doing whatever he wanted, utterly bewitched by his spell.

Three defenders all turned and raced back to shut the door to the goal. There was a split second of opportunity…

So did he belt the ball instantly there and then? Did he hit and hope? No chance. He took one final touch, and as the keeper sprang off his line to make the save, Jamie picked his spot. Then, with perfect timing and a soft touch, he used the outside of his left boot to simply caress the ball home, finding the corner of the net with a strike of almost poetic beauty.

The stadium could have collapsed with the mountain of noise that erupted within it.

Jamie, his heart beating with the joy of a thousand men, slid on his knees to the corner flag. It was a wicked skid all the way to where he wanted to get. Right over to the Tartan Army!

"And look at Mario Caesar – he doesn't know what's hit him! He may have told his players that Johnson had the heart of a lion, but did he also warn them that he had the touch of a sorcerer? Scotland's number 11 is really starting to open up and dictate this game now.

"Here he is again! Two defenders confront him, but Johnson races between them, eating up the ground with his galloping stride. Another defender comes across, but look at Johnson go! He's just knocked the ball forward and decimated the defender for pace. He's on the rampage now and no one can stay with him! To the byline he goes. Now, can he wrap his foot around the ball and deliver a quality cross at the end of his lung-busting run?"

Jamie looked up and spotted his ponytailed target at the far post. Then he wedged his special left foot around the ball, curling it trademark Jamie Johnson style into the area.

The high cross, just hanging there, was an invitation Duncan Farrell simply couldn't refuse. He was a bowling ball, knocking the defensive skittles out of his way, as he powered towards the ball. Then, exploding into the air like a meteor, he simply launched himself at the ball, putting the full weight of his fourteen-stone body behind his header. It flashed past the keeper and pummelled into the back of the net.

Three defenders were lying bulldozed on the ground. Farrell was still standing tall, hands raised to celebrate his goal and arms open, waiting for his partner in crime to join his celebrations.

As soon as Jamie arrived, Farrell jumped down to the ground and started pulling his arms backwards and forwards. He was laughing and indicated that Jamie should sit behind him and do the same. It looked like the strangest goal celebration that Jamie had seen until he realized what Faz was actually doing – he was rowing!

Jamie leapt down behind him and together they rowed very merrily along the rain-soaked pitch. Soon, the other players were all joining in too. They had no idea that they were reenacting Faz and Jamie's ill-fated midnight trip down the Thames; they only knew Scotland were sensationally navigating their way past Brazil en route to the quarter-finals of the World Cup.

FULL-TIME
Scotland 2 - 1 Brazil
J Johnson, 61   Rodinaldo, 36
D Farrell, 64

Scotland through to the quarter-finals!

"And that is good to see! Even the Brazil fans are applauding the Scotland players as their heroic captain, Cameron McManus, leads them on a lap of the pitch. That's what makes Brazil such a wonderful footballing nation. They appreciate great football – no matter who it's played by. And there, in the centre of the pitch, it looks as though an exchange is taking place between arguably the two best players in the World Cup so far…"

"Hey, Johnson! Mister – we can swap the shirts?"

Jamie turned around. It was Rodinaldo. He wanted to swap shirts with Jamie.

"Sure," said Jamie, taking off his top and handing it over. He was a bit self-conscious that it might be too wet and smelly but really he was just relieved. He'd completely forgotten that he needed to get Rodinaldo's shirt for Robbie. He was lucky that Rodinaldo had come to him.

The two players – one black and one a very pale white – hugged and a million camera flashes went off all at the same time. The pictures were to be on the back of every newspaper the next morning because it was an image that said everything about football and its ability to bring people together no matter where they came from in the world.

"Hey," said Jamie, proudly slipping on Rodinaldo's Brazil shirt. "Your fans. I think they're singing something at me. Can you tell me what they're singing?"

Rodinaldo smiled. He had the biggest, whitest teeth Jamie had ever seen. In truth, he probably needed a brace.

"Ah!" he laughed. "At you, they sing, *'Fenomeno.'* It means they like you. Very much. They say you are a phenomenon."

Basket Case

The mood in the dressing room was euphoric.

The players could still hear the fans outside singing:

Now you're gonna believe us,
Now you're gonna believe us,
Now you're gonna beliee-eeve us...
We're gonna win the Cup!

WE'RE GONNA WIN THE CUP ...
WE'RE GONNA WIN THE CUP!

The players began singing along too. Now that they had beaten Brazil, who could argue with them?

Ecstasy filled the air. From somewhere a champagne bottle appeared and Allie Stone was just about to open it and spray the contents all over his teammates when he saw the expression on Sir Brian Robertson's face.

"Put the champagne away, Allie," the boss ordered, calmly. "Let's celebrate when we win this tournament. Because that's what we're here to do."

Then Robertson's face darkened and his voice deepened.

"Johnson. Farrell. Meeting. Outside the showers. Now."

Scotland's goal scorers hung their heads and followed their manager over to the private area of the dressing room. Now was the time for his verdict on yesterday's late-night riverside antics.

"Boss," said Jamie, attempting to get his apology in first. "We're really sorry. It will never happen again. Ever."

Farrell nodded in silent agreement.

"You two! *Especially* you," Robertson snarled, looking at Jamie. "After what your body's been through? You two must be the most stupid pair of so -and-sos I've come across in forty years of football."

Robertson stared at his pair of miscreants like a judge about to deliver their sentence, before saying: "But, by Christ, can you both play. Never again, gentlemen. Never again."

Jamie and Faz were just breaking into a smile of

relief when, suddenly, there was a knock on the door. It was the drug-testing officials, making their routine examinations on the players after the game.

Realizing the potential implications of being discovered breaking his dressing room ban, Brian Robertson swiftly manoeuvred himself into the huge red plastic laundry box that was next to the showers.

"Tommy!" he yelled, getting in. "You know what to do."

And with that, Tommy McAvennie put the lid on the container and, assisted by one of the physios, carried the rather heavy box out of the dressing room, right underneath the noses of the drug testers.

"And so that just about rounds off our coverage from White Hart Lane on what proved to be a quite incredible night. It will live long in the memory of anyone who was here to witness it. And Sir Brian Robertson, wherever you are – congratulations! Your boys put in one hell of a performance."

Indeed, from within the very bowels of the stadium, as the Scotland Team back-room staff loaded their equipment on to the team coach, tucked away inside one of the big red boxes was a very happy manager indeed. And he had already begun hatching his plan for the quarter-finals.

⑭

Headlines

FOOTBALL

CharlesSummers
at White Hart Lane

Contenders!

The impossible dream CAN come true

Brian Robertson has said it from the beginning of the tournament. First, he convinced his players that it was true, then the fans saw it was possible and now, having overcome the football superpower that is Brazil, even we cynical souls in the press must start to believe it also.

Before this match, hope had been blurred by doubt – but with this majestic performance, the clouds have been lifted to reveal the bright light of belief.

Other teams may have more talent than this stubborn and yet stylish Scottish side, but surely no one will have a stronger team spirit.

Yes, you may well pinch yourself and read this sentence again: Scotland *can* win the World Cup.

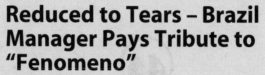

Reduced to Tears – Brazil Manager Pays Tribute to "Fenomeno"

"This is a player of quite exceptional talent," Mario Ceasar said after watching his side be comprehensively dismantled by the wing wonder. "We told our players about Johnson and we'd watched DVDs, but it is only when your defender comes back to the dressing room and he is crying that you understand how powerful this player is."

45

Dumped

Friday 29 June

"Chin up, Jamie. Plenty more fish in the sea, eh?" chuckled Allie Stone, giving Jamie a comforting pat on the back.

Jamie had no idea what he was talking about. He just stared at Stonefish as though he were a looney tune. He'd just played the game of his life, his chin was already up!

But when Jamie walked past Cameron McManus and Owen Tully and they both shook their heads at him in pity, he knew something was up.

And then he saw the front page of the paper.

Johnson Dumped

World Exclusive: Loretta Martin Interview

The personal life of Jamie Johnson continues to be just as dramatic as his topsy-turvy World Cup journey. The day after he inspired Scotland to a historic victory against Brazil (see special Goals pull-out) we can reveal he has now been DUMPED!

"It's over," announced Loretta Martin, who has been linked to Johnson throughout the tournament. In a statement released through her representative last night, the former hairdresser's assistant said: "He's got a World Cup to play in and I've got my own stuff going on too. My agent's been really busy and we've had lots of offers. Jamie Johnson is in the past for me. I'm looking forward to the future."

Do you have a story about a celebrity? Email us for a free cash reward!

Jamie felt like banging his head on the table. He'd been a complete and utter idiot. He'd been warned about gold-diggers and now he knew why. This girl had seen Jamie coming from a mile off and played him like a fool.

It was bad enough that the whole world thought he was some kind of item with a girl he didn't even know. But now they all thought he'd been dumped by her too. Could his luck with girls get any worse?

At that moment, Jamie suddenly felt a soft hand rest on his shoulder and the subtle scent of perfume nestle in his nostrils.

He looked up to see Diana Budd, the Scotland Team press officer, smiling sweetly at him.

"Are you OK, Jamie?" she asked, nodding sympathetically at the newspaper.

"Yeah," said Jamie. "I'm fine. Just another lesson I've learned the hard way."

"Good… Listen, I know you've done a lot of interviews, but are you OK to do one for me tomorrow afternoon, to preview the quarter-final against South Korea?"

"Sure," said Jamie. "No probs." He liked Diana. She knew loads about football because her dad had been a brilliant international striker for Scotland – one of Mike's favourite players. And, besides, Jamie liked her perfume.

"Thanks! We'll do it at the seating area, by the pool," she said, before adding as if it were just an afterthought: "Oh, Jack Marshall's doing the interview, by the way, and it's live – hope that's OK."

46

Fart Attack

"What's the problem?" said Jamie, looking at Robbie Simmonds' disappointed face. "That's it; I swear that's Rodinaldo's shirt! Look, if you don't want it, I'm sure there'll be plenty of others who will!"

There were just two days before the quarter-final with South Korea and, keen to avoid a repeat of Jamie and Duncan's late-night swim before the last game, Sir Brian Robertson had organized a top stand-up comedian to come into the hotel and do a gig for the squad to keep their minds off the game. It was good stuff – really funny – so Jamie had waited until the break to pop out and meet Robbie in reception to hand over the shirt.

But instead of being overwhelmed with gratitude, Robbie seemed unimpressed. Disappointed, even.

"Nah, it's cool, I'll have it and I appreciate it and all that – must be worth loads on eBay," he said, grabbing the shirt from Jamie's hands. "It's just that I'm over Rodinaldo now. He's yesterday's man."

"Really?" said Jamie. "So who's today's, then?"

"Derrrr!" laughed Robbie. "I'm looking at him!"

Jamie's eyes widened. He was just taking in all the implications of what Robbie was saying when he suddenly heard the wailing sound of sirens roaring up the path outside the hotel.

An ambulance screeched to a halt and two paramedics leapt out and sprinted into the hotel.

They ran straight into the room where the Scotland squad were listening to the comedian.

Jamie burst into the room. A crowd of anxious faces gathered around the paramedics, who were treating someone on the floor.

Jamie had a sick feeling. As soon as he'd seen the ambulance his body had gone freezing cold and his mind had immediately replayed what had happened to Mike. Jamie had only just started to get close to Sir Brian Robertson... He just hoped this wasn't what he thought it was.

"When did he collapse?" the paramedics were asking.

"He was fine, everything was cool – we were just listening to the comedy and he was laughing like everyone else," Tommy, the kit man, was explaining to the paramedics, his face ashen with concern. "And then as soon as there was a break, he just fell off his chair in agony. Just slumped to the floor, kind of thing. Is he going to be OK?"

Jamie moved forward. He had to see who was on the floor. He felt sure he already knew.

"Suspected appendicitis!" one of the paramedics shouted to his colleague, who nodded in agreement.

Jamie looked down and was shocked to see that it was not Sir Brian Robertson, but Allie Stone who was writhing in agony on the floor. The paramedics were feeling the side of his stomach and Jamie had never seen anyone so obviously in such excruciating pain. His mum had told him stories about patients whose appendix had burst on their way to the hospital; he knew how dangerous it could be. Even life-threatening.

"OK, we're bringing him in," the paramedic shouted into a walkie-talkie. "Tell A&E we'll be there in five minutes. We'll need the anaesthetist ready on arrival."

They delicately rolled Allie Stone – who was almost in tears with the pain – on to his side and began to lift him on to the stretcher.

But the moment they clasped their hands around his

waist, a quite thunderous noise emitted from Allie's rear end. It must have lasted for about ten seconds, but it was impossible to tell exactly how long. Time seemed to stand still as the deep sound continued to fill the room while everyone just looked at one another, mystified, trying to work out what on earth was going on.

The instant the noise stopped, Allie Stone suddenly leapt back to his feet, looking like a new man.

"Oooh," he said, rubbing his stomach. "Better out than in! Right, let's get on with this gig!"

The two paramedics, without saying another word, simply packed up their equipment and started to make their way out of the room and back to the ambulance.

"Contact A&E," one of them said into her walkie-talkie as they left the hotel. "Tell them to stand down the emergency situation from this end. Just a severe case of trapped wind."

47

The Professionals

Saturday 30 June – two days before the quarter-final

"Anyone seen my pants?" said Allie Stone in the hotel changing room. The players had all gone for a swim in the outdoor pool to keep their muscles loose ahead of the match against South Korea and now Allie Stone was wandering around naked, looking in everyone's bags.

"Get away, you tube, or I'll knock your block off!" shouted Duncan Farrell. "Why do you think I'd nick your pants anyway? They'll only be full of skid marks."

"All right, Faz," laughed Allie. "Come on then, you lot – own up. Who's got my pants?"

Jamie chuckled as he went outside to do his

interview. These guys didn't feel like teammates any more. They felt like brothers.

Jack was already waiting a few yards away by the pool. She was wearing jeans and a tight white top, which was shimmering in the afternoon sun.

"Hi, Jamie," she said, taking off her sunglasses and reaching out her hand to shake his. "Thanks for doing this."

"No problem," said Jamie, sitting down.

He couldn't remember the last time he'd shaken Jack's hand.

"So how's the knee holding up, Jamie?" asked Jack, once the cameras were rolling.

"Yeah, it's fine, thanks," Jamie lied. He didn't want Jack the journalist or Jack the friend to know what he was doing to his body to still be playing in this tournament. He was hardly training in between games now. Once the injections wore off sometimes the pain was almost unbearable.

"Good ... because we heard rumours that there was an ambulance called to the hotel last night?"

"Oh, don't believe everything you hear – just a load of hot air," said Jamie, laughing inside at his own joke.

"And what about Sir Brian Robertson? They're starting to call him The Miracle Man in the press for what he's achieving with this team. What do you make of him?"

"I think the press are right!" beamed Jamie. "His football brain is amazing. It's like a kind of cross between a computer and a camera. He doesn't miss a thing."

"So would you say that he has become something of a father figure to you?"

Jamie paused for a second. He rubbed his ringless finger, feeling his pulse quicken as it always did whenever the words "dad" or "father" were mentioned. And then, as he thought about his answer, a sense of calm washed over him.

"Yes," he smiled, realizing perhaps for the first time why he liked playing for Robertson so much. "I guess he is. He knows how to handle me, anyway."

"So, with Sir Brian in charge, and now a very winnable game against South Korea in the quarters, is there a feeling in the dressing room that you can go all the way to the final?"

"Why not?" responded Jamie. "We believe we can win. We are a tight unit and we're full of belief. And I've got to say that this is by far the most serious and dedicated group of professionals I've ever played with—"

"Anyone seen my pants?!" A loud and familiar voice suddenly said.

Jamie, Jack and the TV camera all turned around to focus on Allie Stone standing by the pool, completely naked, with only his hands to protect his modesty. Not that he was embarrassed. Not one bit.

"Oops!" he smiled. "Not interrupting, am I?"

"Stonefish! We're doing an interview! It's live!" Jamie said through tightly clenched teeth. He was beginning to see Stonefish's naked body a little more often than he liked!

"Oops!" Stonefish repeated before giving a big thumbs up straight to the camera. "Hiya, Mum! Hiya, Gran! OK, well, let me know if any of you see my pants!"

And with that, he turned and left, revealing his big, podgy bum to the nation for good measure.

"Erm, sorry about that," mumbled Jamie, trying to regain his composure. "And, on behalf of the squad, can I just apologize to everyone at home... No one wants to see that ... erm... What were we talking about?"

"I think you were just saying that this was the most serious and dedicated group of professionals you'd ever played with!" answered Jack, trying to hold in her laughter.

"Oh, right, yeah..." said Jamie, realizing that Allie Stone's bum had kind of put pay to that claim.

Now they were both laughing. Just like the good old days when they'd been kids at school. Finally, it took Jack to get the interview back on track.

"OK, last question, Jamie: how would you say you've adapted your game to suit the international stage? Are you doing anything different now you're playing at the World Cup?"

Jamie shook his head.

"I'm just doing what I love," he smiled. "I still try and play the same way that I did when I was a kid having a kick around with my best friend back home in Sunningdale Park."

Jamie looked closely at Jack for a reaction. You could never tell with her. She had a great poker face and her dark skin colour meant she didn't go red. But Jamie could have sworn he saw her blush.

"Sorry about Allie Stone," said Jamie after the end of the interview. "You got more than you bargained for there, didn't you?"

"Yeah, well, as a journalist I'm always trying to get to the naked truth."

Jack laughed and so did Jamie. It was great to see her smile again. Maybe his luck was about to change.

"OK, then. Thanks, Jamie," said Jack, reaching out her hand again to say goodbye.

But Jamie didn't want to shake her hand. And he didn't want her to leave either.

"Listen, Jack," he said, reaching forward to touch her

lightly on the shoulder. "Why don't you chill here for a bit and we can—"

But the moment Jamie made contact with her, Jack seemed to turn to ice. Her smile froze into a frown.

"Oh, sorry to hear about you and that girl breaking up," she said, taking a little step back with each word that came out of her mouth. "She seemed like a really *nice* girl."

"What?!" growled Jamie, furious that Loretta Martin was coming between him and Jack again. "I was never with that stupid gold-digger! I don't even know her! I knew you wouldn't believe me!"

"OK, Jamie, calm down," said Jack, putting her sunglasses back on. "Wow – I guess you must have really liked her."

And then Jack walked away from Jamie without looking back once.

Marked Man

Monday 2 July – World Cup quarter-final

Scotland 0 - 0 South Korea
24 minutes played

"And if you've just joined us, don't worry, you haven't missed a great deal. There have been precious few clear-cut chances, with the game yet to really spring to life.

"For the first time in the entire tournament, Scotland have been cast as clear favourites in this game, and yet that role does not seem to suit them.

"And you have to say that Jamie Johnson, the jewel in their team who stood out like a shining star in the last round against Brazil, today looks like the invisible man."

*

Jamie stood looking at the two South Korean players surrounding him. He'd not been double-marked like this since he'd been at school. Both players had followed his every step since the kick-off. They were like robots. He felt sure that if he left the pitch right now and went to the toilet, they would both follow him there too!

Although it had hardly been uplifting to hear all the doubts and scorn with which the press and fans had greeted him and his team at the beginning of the tournament, it had at least meant that there was no pressure.

But now, after they had beaten Brazil and Jamie had supposedly proven that he was better than Rodinaldo, the pressure was right on him. And the weight of expectation was a heavy burden to carry.

Scotland 0 - 0 South Korea
HALF-TIME

Brian Robertson had gone absolutely apoplectic: chucking tea cups across the dressing room, shouting in his players' faces; at one point he'd even thrown the whole fruit basket at Duncan Farrell, accusing him of not trying hard enough.

It was a truly frightening few minutes and Robertson was making his point abundantly clear to his team. This performance was unacceptable.

It was only as the buzzer went in the dressing room to signal that the second half was about to start that he finally calmed down.

"OK, so what are we going to do?" asked Brian Robertson, his face still flushed with anger. "You tell me."

Silence. No one said a word. They didn't dare.

"Come on, you lot are supposed to be international footballers, yet we've just played a half of some of the worst football I've ever seen. So, come on, tell me, what's the problem?"

Still no one was prepared to break ranks and give his opinion. The only noise was the persistent thud of Duncan Farrell smacking the side of his own head against the dressing room wall.

Finally, the skipper, Cameron McManus, stood up.

"We've not had this type of game before, boss," he said. "Normally, we're the ones defending. But this lot are just sitting behind the ball. When we've got the ball, we look up and every single one of our players is marked. Jamie's got two men on him the whole time. We can't play through 'em, boss."

"Of course you can't play through them," said Robertson. "It's impossible. So what do you do instead? You play around them."

Jamie could sense Robertson's fury turning to

236

animation as he marched towards the tactics board in the corner of the dressing room.

"Look," he said. "Remember when you were at school, playing in the playground? You'd have a defender in front of you, so you'd flick the ball against the wall, go around the player and then collect the ball again on the other side?"

The dressing room nodded their heads as one. They'd all used that trick at school.

"Well, that's what we do now. Just use a teammate as the wall, like this…"

He drew a diagram on the board.

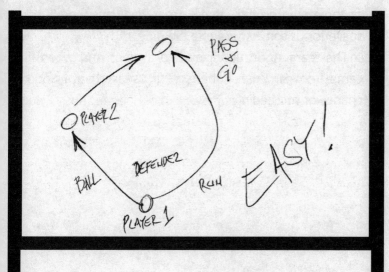

"The wall pass, push and go, quick one two ... whatever you want to call it. That's the way to break down their team. Keep it simple, keep it first time and keep it quick. They won't be able to stay with you. OK?"

Again the dressing room agreed.

"And Jamie, yes you've got two men on you, but you know what? That's fine. In fact, it's good. See if you can make it three. When you get the ball, pause for a second, tease them, draw them in. You'll be like a magnet to the markers and then, when you're surrounded, switch the ball quickly – if Jamie's got two or three men on him, that's great. It means there'll be space for us somewhere else. So use it!"

The team stood up. They had a plan. And when it came from Sir Brian Robertson, it usually had a good chance of succeeding.

True Leader

Jamie joined in the joyous celebration, leaping on Duncan Farrell's back, dragging the big striker down to the ground as if he were felling a giant oak.

Jamie was fully aware that he had not touched the ball once during the whole glorious move that had led to the goal. But he couldn't care less. He knew that he had still done his bit. By staying away from the ball and keeping the attention of the defenders with him, he had played his part.

Scotland 1 - 0 South Korea
D Farrell. 70

At the time of the goal, it had appeared that Scotland might just cruise into the semi-finals. Robertson's men had started enjoying themselves – spraying the ball freely around the pitch while, in the stands, the Tartan Army were getting ready to celebrate.

But just minutes later a sickening clash of heads between Cameron McManus and the South Korean striker brought Scotland crashing back down to earth.

The clash of heads was so loud that it sounded as though McManus might have even crushed his skull in the collision.

And when he stood up, his teammates could see the full extent of the damage that had been done.

Blood was pouring from a gash in his forehead as if from a tap, and his right eye was already swelling up like a boxer that has taken a pummelling for twelve rounds.

The doctor and physio immediately came on to the pitch and led McManus away down the tunnel. His shirt was now stained a dark claret colour. Jamie wondered how his captain could have any blood left inside his body, such was the volume of the liquid pumping out from the wound.

Which made it all the more surprising when, only four minutes later, McManus re-emerged from the tunnel, his head swathed with bandages, impatiently gesturing to the ref to let him come back on the pitch.

Word quickly went round that the medics had found a way of temporarily gluing McManus's wound together after he'd flatly dismissed the possibility of his coming off. Being substituted was never an option for him. He was captain of his country. They would have to cut off his leg before he stopped playing for Scotland.

They'd bandaged him up to play out this match, but the wound was so bad that after this he'd need to head straight to the hospital and have about twenty stitches. He'd have a huge scar for the rest of his life and there was little doubt that he'd be out of the semi-final if Scotland got through.

It was a personal tragedy for the skipper but, if anything, that knowledge seemed to just inspire McManus to greater heights.

He seemed to work harder, and become yet more focused on getting Scotland over the line.

In those last ten minutes, he became a man mountain. Stopping every attack with a definitive display of defensive determination. Even when the moment came for him to win a header, he didn't shirk it, despite the fact that the ball smashed into the very place where, under the bandages, his head was little more than a gaping hole.

When the final whistle went, McManus collapsed. He'd been playing through the pain barrier. He'd just wanted to get Scotland through before he allowed his body to give in.

As his teammates went to surround and congratulate McManus, Jamie understood there were different ways of leading a team. Some players talked, some players shouted. And others led by example. McManus was one of the latter.

He'd put the team first.

Now that's a proper captain, Jamie thought to himself as McManus raised his battered body from the floor to lead his players around the pitch to applaud the Tartan Army for their unswerving support. *And he didn't even have to say a word*.

WORLD CUP QUARTER-FINAL
FULL-TIME
Scotland 1   -   0 South Korea
D Farrell, 70

Quarter-Final Results

Scotland 1-0 South Korea
Argentina 3-1 Germany

England 4-3 Spain
Holland 2-1 Turkey

Semi-Finals

6 July
Argentina v Scotland
Old Trafford
KICK-OFF 8 p.m.

7 July
England v Holland
The Emirates
KICK-OFF 8 p.m.

50

Press

FOOTBALL

Charles Summers
at Villa Park

Tide Turns For Scotland

Starting with big Allie Stone, almost every player on the side had a touch of the ball as the attack flowed into the opposition half – picking up pace along the way. Each pass was played as swiftly as possible, with the ball being laid into space for the onrushing teammate to gather in at top speed.

Like a wave gathering momentum as it rushes towards the shore, Scotland's attack raced towards the South Korean goal with devastating and irresistible danger. All the cogs and mechanisms of Brian Robertson's well-oiled machine clicked into place and, as Duncan Farrell applied the final, crucial, crushing touch to the move, poking the ball home from close range, the manager was up from his seat, applauding his team, who had brought his vision of the beautiful game to life.

History!

Robertson's boys march into the semis!

Scotland last night reached the final four of the World Cup for the first time in their history … to set up a mouth-watering return match against Argentina.

port

MCK

Brave McManus plays on after gruesome clash of heads

Scotland skipper rushed to hospital after the game for emergency plastic surgery on gaping wound.

Best

Next Stage

Tuesday 3 July – three days before
World Cup semi-final v Argentina

"Of course I'm sure," said Sir Brian Robertson. "It's the right time for you."

Robertson had a way of talking that made Jamie feel that even if he went out on to the pitch by himself to take on the best team in the world, he would still be able to give them a good old thrashing. He gave Jamie the belief that he could do absolutely anything.

But this. This was something else. It had taken Jamie completely by surprise.

He stood up and started pacing around the room, rubbing his finger where his ring should have been.

"But I've never been captain of any team," Jamie said, panicking at the prospect. "People always said I didn't shout enough on the pitch or that you can't be a captain if you're a wing—"

"Well, I don't care what other people have said," stated Robertson. "I've been a manager for nearly forty years, so I think I know what I'm doing by now. It's only for one game, Jamie. McManus will be ready for the next one."

"But boss, I'm only eighteen; there are players in this squad in their thirties. How can I captain them? How do you know they'll respect me?"

"Trust me, Jamie. I can see it in their eyes. When they can see you on the pitch on *their* side, they believe. You give them that belief. It's time for the next stage in your career, Jamie. It's time for you to become a leader."

Robertson paused, weighing up his final decision.

"Just answer me one question, Jamie. Do you want to do it? Do you want to captain your country?"

Jamie nodded and said three words. "I'm dying to."

(52)

Cruising

Wednesday 4 July – two days before World Cup semi-final v Argentina

From: **Mum**

To: JJ[JJ@JamieJohnson.info]

Date:

Subject:

Jamie – got your text about being captain! That's amazing! Cruise is great, by the way. I've told everyone on board that I'm your mum but hardly anyone believes me! Anyway, we're in Greece now. It's absolutely roasting here. What's it like there? Make sure you wear lots of suntan lotion when you're playing outside, please. You know how easily you get burnt. We can watch all the games here, too. By the way, I didn't go to the toilet for your goal against Brazil … but Jeremy did! So he's taking all the credit! He says he's going to drink loads of orange juice a couple of hours before the game against Argentina. Maybe you'll get a cat-trick!

Anyway, seriously, Jamie, I know I'm no footy expert. I don't know how you do those overhead fouls, or how

248

the onside rule works, but I do know that captaining your country is the best thing you could ever do. And I know that, somewhere, your granddad is the proudest man in the world. (You already have the proudest mum!)

Call me when you can after the game,

Luv m & j xxxxxxx

Jamie smiled. He was definitely right to have texted her the news. He could tell from her email that if he'd done it over the phone, she would have burst into floods of tears. He liked making her proud, though, and he hoped that she could remember everything he had achieved when he eventually plucked up the courage to tell her that he had lost the ring. He knew that she would probably be even more upset than him.

Ever since he'd lost it, Jamie's mind had been haunted by the memory of the day his mum had given it to him. It had been soon after Mike had died.

"Dad wanted you to have this," she had told Jamie, handing him the gold band. "He always said that you had more pride in your little finger than any man he ever met. He wanted you to wear this ring with pride, and to pass it on to your own son."

How could he tell his mum that he'd lost it? What

would he say? The words just wouldn't come out of his mouth. And the worst part was that everything he was achieving at this World Cup was tainted for him by the fact that he'd lost it.

Jamie took a deep breath and closed his eyes. Then he read the email once more before logging out. He knew that there were some lines in there that would cheer him up.

Overhead foul? The onside rule? Cat-trick?!

Where did she get this stuff from? Honestly! Was she taking the mickey?! After all these years, and both a dad and a son who were obsessed with the game, she still didn't know any of the football lingo? *Right*, Jamie thought to himself, *time to sort this out.*

JJ's Football Dictionary! Your way to sound like you know football.

(Mum – please learn all of these – I'm serious! I will be testing you!!)

Offside Rule

Right, actually thinking about this, I'm going to have to explain this to you when I see you next. All we need is some salt and pepper pots and I'll show you on the kitchen table. It's simple. In the meantime, though, please don't ever refer to the "onside rule". It's "OFFside!" Please remember that – repeat 1000 times if you have to!

Rainbow Flick

This is when you flick the ball over your own head in a looping curve. (That's why it's called rainbow, Mum!!) Makes a mug of the defenders and looks soooo cool. Try it – I bet you'll never be able to do it! But I can!!

Hat-Trick

When you score three goals – brilliant achievement for any player! Not, under any circumstance to be confused with a "cat-trick!" Don't even know where you got that one from, Mum! What kind of tricks do you even do with a cat?! You've made a paw mistake there! Ha ha!!! Seriously, you must be the only person in the world who doesn't know what a hat-trick is!!

Around the World

No, not a cruise like the one you're on now!! This is when you are keeping the ball up and while the ball's already in the air, you quickly move your kicking foot up and around the top of the ball, in a circle, getting it back underneath the ball in time to kick it up again. Cos your foot goes in a circle, it's called "Around the World". See how clever football is, _mum_! I can't draw but it looks like this:

TOLD YOU I COULDN'T DRAW

Overhead Kick (NOT OVERHEAD FOUL!)

This is the most wicked skill and also one of the hardest! Scissor-kicking the ball above your head in mid-air. Remember I did it and scored a goal with it when I was mascot for Hawkstone? People still ask me about that one!

Nuts!

If you hear me shouting this during a game, then you know I've done something good! Cos this is what you shout when you kick the ball between someone's legs. It's called a "nutmeg" but it only properly counts if you remember to shout "nuts!" when you do

Jamie's phone rang, which was annoying as he was actually really enjoying writing his football dictionary. Not only would it finally be the answer to his mum always making the most embarrassing comments at football matches ("Kick it hard, Jamie! Really kick it right into the goal!") but it was also a fun way to relax ahead of the Argentina game. He let the phone ring out but then it started up again almost immediately.

Jamie put down his pen and picked up his phone.

It was Jack. Again. This was the fourth time she'd called since yesterday. Even though he was desperate to tell her that he'd been made captain for the semi-final, he wasn't interested in talking to her if it meant another verbal battle.

Having another row with Jack right now, so close to such a titanic match, was the last thing he needed. He'd get all tongue-tied and his words wouldn't come out properly and he'd forget all the stuff that he wanted to say. It was always the same with her.

He'd been thinking about Jack a lot over the last couple of days – even more than usual – and he'd realized why the argument they'd had after the interview by the pool had upset him so much. It wasn't the fact that she'd teased him for being dumped. It wasn't even the fact that she didn't want him to touch her. It was that she'd actually believed that he was interested in another girl.

Jack was supposed to be the clever one out of the two of them. So how was it that, after all this time, she still hadn't managed to work out the fact that, for Jamie, there *were* no other girls?

He took a final look at her name flashing up on his phone and then put it on silent.

53

Destiny Calling

Thursday 5 July – one day before World Cup semi-final v Argentina – Scotland manager and captain give joint press conference

"Yes, we've lost McManus, but Jamie's the perfect man to take on the captaincy for this game," said Sir Brian Robertson, while ten different translators spun his words into different languages for the journalists who had assembled from around the world.

"Leadership is not about age, it's about respect, and believe you me, my lads respect Jamie.

"Speaking of respect, I also think it's really important that Ricardo Barron has been appointed referee for this match. This game needs a strong official, someone who is clear in his own mind and takes no rubbish and Barron is certainly that man. For me, he's the best referee in the world and he'll be one of the most important people on that pitch tomorrow night."

"People are making Argentina favourites for the game. Brian, do you agree with that?" asked a reporter.

"Couldn't care less. The only thing that is important is my players. If they believe in themselves as much as I believe in them, then there's nothing we can't achieve. If we've proved anything so far, it's that we have nothing to fear."

"And Jamie, it looks like Bertorelli is going to be named captain for Argentina," said another journalist with a smile. "Can you tell us if you've forgiven him for the foul in the group game? People called it the tackle from hell."

Jamie threw a toxic look at the journalist. He knew that in life you were supposed to forgive and forget, but what Bertorelli had done to him – taunting him while he lay stricken in agony on the ground – there was no way he could forgive anyone for that. As he thought back to that day, he could feel his anger rise and multiply inside him. So, no, of course he hadn't forgiven Bertorelli for the tackle. It was the complete opposite; Jamie wanted revenge. And he wanted it badly.

"I'm not answering that question," he said, finally. "I don't want to get involved."

Jamie heard his phone vibrate on his bedside table. It was two o'clock in the morning but he was still wide awake. He had so much nervous energy that he felt as if he could go out right now and run a marathon – if his knee was up to it.

They had said in the press conference that they expected a worldwide TV audience of seven hundred million people for tomorrow's game. Jamie didn't even know how many zeros that was.

He picked up his phone and rolled on to his back. There was a text waiting for him.

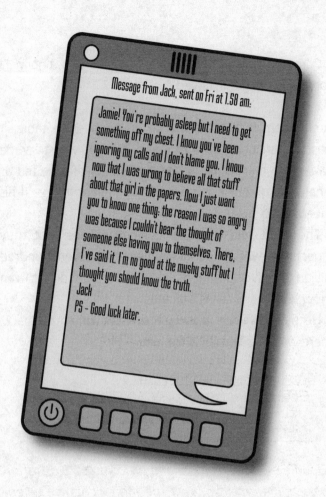

Message from Jack, sent on Fri at 1.58 am:

Jamie! You're probably asleep but I need to get something off my chest. I know you've been ignoring my calls and I don't blame you. I know now that I was wrong to believe all that stuff about that girl in the papers. Now I just want you to know one thing: the reason I was so angry was because I couldn't bear the thought of someone else having you to themselves. There, I've said it. I'm no good at the mushy stuff but I thought you should know the truth.
Jack
PS – Good luck later.

Jamie read the words again. Then he closed his eyes and shook his head. Jack was wrong.

She *was* good at the mushy stuff.

Moment
of Truth

***Friday 6 July – match day,
World Cup semi-final***

WORLD CUP SEMI-FINAL
Scotland v Argentina
Old Trafford
KICK-OFF 8 p.m.

"Good evening, everyone, and welcome to Old Trafford for a game which has all the ingredients of an epic drama. Two teams, evenly matched, tantalizingly only one game away from the World Cup Final.

"Two years ago, Jamie Johnson was told his football career was over. Tonight, remarkably, he leads his team out at the World Cup as one of the most talented

259

teenagers around the globe. Football fans are looking forward to seeing the galloping magician play today. And such has been his impact on this tournament that they are hoping, if not expecting, to see something very special from the young man. And there he is, at the front of the tunnel, ready to lead out his team for a match that is going to be watched the world over.

"And if you haven't heard the news, there has been a very late change of officials. Ricardo Barron, acknowledged as the best referee in the world, unfortunately went down late last night with a severe dose of food poisoning. He is to be replaced by the man who was due to be the Fourth Official, Giovanni Fattifachi. We understand that Sir Brian Robertson is deeply unhappy about this late change, but there is no suggestion of foul play.

"But back to the football, and let's show you those all-important team line-ups again…

"And now the two captains meet in the centre circle to toss the coin. And there's no other way to say this – although they are both great players, they have made no secret of the animosity between them.

"So the moment of truth now… And Bertorelli stretches out his hand and – oh that is surprising! This time it's Johnson who refuses to shake! Now this must go back to the tackle the Argentinian made during the

4-4-2

Stone

Renton   Craig   Tulley   Miller

Baxter   Gray   Niven   Johnson (c)

McCall

Farrell

Hurricco   Madistuta   Revez

Bertorelli (c)

Rocha   Cruz   Taldano

Pavon   Rattin   Labatoni

Ortega

3-3-1-3

group match between these two sides, which almost put Johnson out of the World Cup.

"And look at Johnson's face – just look at that – the real anger on his face! He does not like Bertorelli one bit. That's certainly going to be one to keep an eye on.

"Well, it looks like we're already off and running and a ball has not even been kicked yet! Stay with us because you won't want to miss this one. And it's all here … LIVE!"

As the match kicked off, Jamie opened his nostrils and drew in a lungful of air. He had never felt so alive.

As captain of his country, he'd led his team in singing the national anthem, belting out every word of "Flower of Scotland" with all the pride in his heart and now, with the Tartan Army in their full, majestic voice, he was ready to do anything – whatever it took – to win this game for them.

Argentina – or, to be precise, their goalkeeper – soon felt the full force of Duncan Farrell. As he leapt to contest a trademark Jamie Johnson centre, Farrell bashed Diego Ortega out of his way, sending him crashing into his own net, before the big striker headed home.

Scotland and Farrell had landed the first blow, and maybe in the Premier League the strike might have been allowed to stand, but the ear-piercing shriek of the referee's whistle clearly indicated that he'd disallowed the goal.

And that was just the start.

Perhaps Giovanni Fattifachi was being sponsored for every blow of his whistle. He couldn't resist it; even the slightest infringement resulted in that high-pitched peep. *Peep! Peep! Peep!* With his arm stretched dramatically above his head and an overly serious expression on his face. It was as though he imagined he was being marked for the quality, volume and artistic merit of each blow of his whistle. Was he scared that if he didn't blow it every five seconds it would stop working? Did he think he was the star of the show? Certainly he appeared to have no interest in letting the game flow.

Fussy? The man probably picked the seeds off his strawberries.

Fattifachi, a very thin, wiry, hairy man, was blowing up every time a Scotland player went in for a tackle and yet he was missing all the dirty little tricks that the Argentinians were pulling. An honest tackle from a Scotland player was called a foul and treated like a heinous crime, yet the shirt-pulling, ankle taps and, worse still, the stray elbows of the Argentinians were all allowed to go unpunished.

And worst of all was the fact that Fattifachi seemed

quite content to have conversations and even a laugh with the Argentinian players in Spanish and yet the only English words he seemed to know were: "Foul" and "I am the referee, not you!"

Predictably, the harshest of the Argentinians' treatment was reserved for Jamie. He was playing well; full of running and confidence, but so far the Argentinians had managed to contain him. Just.

If they weren't jostling and jabbing him every time he got on the ball, they were tripping him, body checking him, and poking him in the eye. Pavon even bit Jamie's ear! But they made sure that the same player never fouled Jamie twice in succession. They took it in turns so they didn't get booked. It was a cruel tactic but also clever.

Scotland 0 - 0 Argentina
HALF-TIME

"Are you OK, Jamie?" asked Sir Brian Robertson at the end of his team talk. "Remember the fact that they are targeting you is really the ultimate compliment."

Jamie looked at his ribs. He had an indentation of four stud marks on his torso. How did anyone manage to find his ribs when they were aiming for the ball? His shirt was torn and his socks had a hole in them from which blood was seeping out.

"I know, boss," he smiled. "But they'll have to do more than that to get rid of me."

Scotland 0 - 0 Argentina
SECOND-HALF

"Well, we're just waiting for the players to come back out on to the pitch and get this semi-final back under way. And you can't help thinking that there are a few more twists and turns left in this game. It's a compelling drama and the best part about it is that there's no script!"

The Argentinians seemed to have been given only one instruction at half-time: stop Jamie Johnson. At all costs.

Their plan now seemed ominously clear. They were going to remove Jamie from the game.

If they were playing dirty before, they now took proceedings to an entirely new level.

Sitting on the bench, watching Jamie be spat at for the seventh time, Sir Brian Robertson buried his head in his hands. He just hoped that Jamie would keep his composure. If he lost his temper and got sent off, there would be no way back for Scotland.

But he needn't have worried on that score. Jamie was wound up. In fact, he'd never been so wound up in his life, but he wasn't going to punch anyone. He'd already decided on a far better way of gaining retribution.

The next time he received the ball, he looked up and saw Bertorelli tanking towards him. Jamie stood still. Waiting... Then he knocked the ball cleanly through Bertorelli's legs, shouted proudly "NUTS!" before proceeding to race away from the hugely embarrassed Argentinian captain.

Now, at top speed, Jamie faked to shoot but then continued to drive into the area, side-stepping the last defender.

With the crowd roaring and on their feet, Jamie let rip with a piledriver of a shot, which exploded off his foot and soared with the power of a hurricane into the top corner of the net.

"Oh he's done it! He HAS done it! What a stunning talent this boy is – with the ball at his feet, he is a force of nature – quite simply irresistible! And with that goal, in a World Cup semi-final, Jamie Johnson has surely written his name for ever in the history of football!"

Scotland 1 - 0 Argentina
J Johnson. 58

Jamie ran straight to the Tartan Army. They'd had a difficult start – but now he and the fans were as one.

"How do you like me now?!" he roared at the fans,

kissing his Scotland badge and leaping into the air to punch the sky.

The celebrations were joyous. Faz joined Jamie for another rendition of their "rowing" routine and even Sir Brian Robertson was standing on the touchline waiting to give Jamie a high five.

Scotland were 1-0 up and Jamie had proved the majesty of his skills once more. But there was also a problem: striking the ball with all his might, Jamie had twisted his knee. Not disastrously, but painfully all the same. And there was still half an hour left of the game.

The Final Straight

Scotland 1	-	0 Argentina

J Johnson, 58
75 Minutes Played

Jamie looked at the scoreboard.

Not long now. If they could do it, if they could see this one through, then a World Cup Final lay ahead. A World Cup Final! And a match versus either Holland or … England.

Jamie started to imagine the magnitude of a potential match against England. Against the team that he had so nearly played for… A World Cup Final against the hosts. Nothing could be bigger.

Perhaps he was not the only one whose mind had

started to drift elsewhere because, almost without warning, Argentina made a late break into Scotland's box, and as Allie Stone raced off his line to collect the ball, he was just beaten to it by the Argentinian striker. The attacker made the most of what minimal contact there was, throwing his body dramatically into the air and contorting it like a dying swan.

The referee bought it and immediately whistled. He pointed dramatically to the spot.

"Oh, and we've got unbelievable drama here at Old Trafford. Right at the last minute. So, Mattheus Bertorelli picks up the ball and prepares to place it on the spot. The Scotland fans behind the goal are booing as loud as they can to try to put the striker off but he seems deeply focused on his task. And look at this, the Scotland skipper, Jamie Johnson, is having a quick word in his goalkeeper's ear. I wonder what he's saying. Seems to be some form of advice. Allie Stone nods his head and, as the referee tells Johnson to get out of the area, Bertorelli places the ball carefully down on the penalty spot.

"So here he comes now... This kick to equalize and take the game into extra time and, oh look at Allie Stone, what's he— But it's worked! He's saved it! Allie Stone – well, there's no other way to put

this – has shown Bertorelli his rear-end and Bertorelli has fired the ball straight at it, hitting Stone's bottom, sending it high over the bar. What a way to save a penalty! That is phenomenal. Has there ever been anything like it?! And now Stone is being besieged by his celebrating teammates… He really is the hero of the hour. But wait! The referee doesn't seem happy – oh, he's showing Stone the yellow card. That must be for ungentlemanly conduct. And he's asking for the penalty kick to be retaken!"

The Scotland Team surrounded the referee.

"That's a joke," they shouted.

"How much are they paying you?!"

But Fattifachi shooed them away. He was never going to change his mind.

Bertorelli smiled as he placed the ball back down on the penalty spot. And this time he made no mistake. He put Stone and Scotland to the sword by smashing the ball home into the bottom left-hand corner.

And, in doing so, he took the game into extra time.

Scotland 1 - 1 Argentina
J Johnson, 58   M Bertorelli, 85 pen

MATCH GOES TO EXTRA TIME
15 Minutes Each way

The Scotland players slumped to the ground. They cradled their heads in their hands. Very many of them were verging on tears.

They had been so close. Minutes away. The World Cup Final had been there, waiting for them … calling them … and now it had been snatched away. They had to start all over again.

Jamie lay flat on the ground, panting. He had phenomenal stamina. In all the fitness tests, he always came out on top, and he never, ever got tired during games. But now, all of a sudden, he felt drained of all energy. Completely empty.

And that was when Sir Brian Robertson strolled on to the pitch like a man out for a Sunday afternoon walk.

With an easy smile, Robertson stood above his crestfallen team and, after a second's silence, he took complete charge of the situation.

"OK," he said. "Forget what's just happened. Forget it completely. What I want you to remember is why you all started playing football. When you each kicked your first ball, all of you dreamed of being here, right where you are now. You are thirty minutes away from a World Cup Final. People are watching this match all over the world and every single one of them is asking themselves the same question: how are Scotland going to react to this? Have they got what it takes? And you know what the answer is? You're damn well right we have.

"Right. How is everyone feeling? Everyone OK?"

All the players nodded.

"Jamie? How's the knee?"

"Yeah, it's fine, thanks, boss."

Jamie felt a pang of guilt as he lied, but he couldn't help it. His pride wouldn't allow him to give up now and besides, every cell in his body told him this was it. There would never be another chance like this in his career.

"Good," said Sir Brian. "Then I'll make my last change. Pat, you come off. We'll bring on Bobby Stewart and go 3-4-3. That should allow us to compete better in the midfield. OK, boys, remember: you've proved that you are better than them once. Now go out and do it again."

And with that, Robertson sauntered back across the turf to the touchline. He did not glance back at his team even once. It was time for them to stand on their own two feet.

The Scotland players looked at one another, each one seeing the fire of ambition burning in the others.

Slowly they raised themselves from the ground, a new surge of belief beginning to course through them.

Jamie Johnson looked at his teammates and realized

there was no other group of people he would rather be with for the battle they were about to re-enter.

"Boys," he shouted. "This is it! This is our time. Let's make it happen! WINNERS!!"

Scotland 1   -   1 Argentina
J Johnson, 58   M Bertorelli, 85 pen
EXTRA TIME

"And so we enter extra time of this epic encounter. It has been a splendid see-saw of a game. But which way will it ultimately tip?"

After the thrilling culmination of the first ninety minutes, extra time was cagey. Very cagey. Both teams were equally tired but fully determined not to concede a losing goal, making it all but inevitable that a nail-biting penalty shoot-out would be required to separate the two sides.

However, with five minutes left, Bertorelli got on the ball and, sensing the weariness that had now set into the Scotland side, he went for it.

A path opened up for him right through the centre and he raced through it. Jamie quickly saw the danger. As Bertorelli broke through, charging menacingly towards the penalty area, Jamie raced back to cut him off.

Bertorelli was probably the only Argentinian player capable of going all the way, but Jamie also knew that he was the one player on the Scotland side capable of stopping him.

It was time for Jamie to exact his revenge. Finally, he could deal with his nemesis once and for all.

He'd take the man and the ball.

And this time Bertorelli would feel the pain.

Using every bit of his extraordinary pace, Jamie hunted Bertorelli down like a leopard. He prepared himself to make the lunge … to launch himself into Bertorelli. And that was the moment it went.

Jamie suddenly pulled up and toppled to the ground. His knee had locked and gone. Just at the moment when he most needed it, it had given way completely.

Bertorelli took one quick look over his shoulder and, with what sounded like a laugh, accelerated away towards the goal.

There was no way any other player was going to catch him and, what was worse, there was no way he was ever going to miss.

He dummied to shoot, leaving Allie Stone sprawling on the ground before dribbling the ball right up to the goal line, where he detonated the final, deadly touch.

Bertorelli had scored against Scotland. Again.

Jamie felt himself being hauled off the ground.

He was a broken puppet as he was being carried off the pitch. His body had been kicked and hacked at; his leg was punctured by a series of gaping wounds. Bertorelli and his buddies had aimed to kick Jamie out of the World Cup. And now their wish had been granted.

As Jamie was carried away on the stretcher, he saw his teammates' faces dropping, their belief dissolving, their hope disappearing. He pressed his eyes shut. No tears. Not now. Not in front of them.

Jamie was the symbol of this team; he was their leader. As he left the pitch, so too, it seemed, did Scotland's hopes.

"We'll take you straight to the dressing room, so I can have a look at you," said the doctor walking alongside the paramedics. These were Jamie's worst fears realized. "Then we'll go straight on to the hospital."

Soon Jamie was being carried past the dugout. Brian Robertson patted him on the shoulder while brave Cameron McManus, his own head still swathed in bandages, was generously clapping Jamie on his way.

275

But suddenly Jamie gripped the doctor's hand tightly.

"I'm staying on," he declared.

"What do you mean?" said the doctor. "Your knee's completely—"

"I'm captain of this team," insisted Jamie, staggering unsteadily to his feet, the searing pain burning through him. "And they need me."

"Brave as that sounds, Jamie, with one leg, you're really not going to be much use out there. I mean, you can't even run!"

"No," said Jamie, now aware that the referee had just blown to give Scotland a free kick. "But I can still kick a ball."

Seeing Jamie preparing to come back on, The Tartan Army rose as one to applaud and encourage their wounded leader. Meanwhile, standing by the side of the pitch waiting to limp back into the action, Jamie realized that there comes a moment in every player's career which defines him for ever.

He understood that, for him, that moment was now.

Scotland had a free kick. It was twenty-five yards out, just to the right of centre. Perfect for a left-footer. Perfect for Jamie Johnson.

Jamie looked at the goal and the wall in the front. The Argentinians had set up the wall to stop Jamie bending one of his signature left-foot curlers into the near post. However, the truth was that Jamie's left leg was so badly damaged that there was no way he'd be able to take the free kick with that foot.

Jamie limped up to the ball, each step provoking a spear of pain. Then, taking the whole stadium by surprise, he swept his right foot into the strike. He wanted to swerve it with the outside of his boot right into the top, far corner.

Instantly, he knew it was perfect. As he crashed back down to the ground, Jamie saw the ball beautifully curve over the wall, fizzing fabulously to its target. It was a sublime free kick, flashing like lightning through the air. The goalkeeper, covering the other post, had been left marooned on the wrong side of the goal. There was no way he could save it.

As his strike flew in, Jamie was just about to give a colossal roar of delight, when Mattheus Bertorelli, who was standing on the goal line, leapt into the air and punched the ball over the crossbar – with his fist!

"Penalty, ref!" the players shouted and crowded around the referee. "He's got to be sent off!"

But the referee did not see it. Or, if he did, he refused to give it. He simply whistled and pointed to a Scotland corner! The players continued to contest the decision, begging him to consult his linesman, but Fattifachi stubbornly shook his head and booked both Farrell and Tulley for dissent.

Jamie collapsed and crawled off the pitch. He knew now that he had nothing left. That had been his final effort before his body, at long last, surrendered.

All he could do was watch the last agonizing four minutes from the sidelines as Scotland's ten men desperately tried to produce an equalizer.

The clock had only reached a hundred and nineteen minutes and forty seconds when Giovanni Fattifachi, with what looked almost like a satisfied smile, stopped his watch and blew the final whistle on the game.

And, just like that it was finished. Scotland's World Cup journey had come to an end.

It was over.

World Cup Semi-Final

Scotland 1	-	2 Argentina
J Johnson, 58		M Bertorelli, 85 pen, 114
FULL-TIME		

Argentina progress to World Cup Final

Plane Thinking

Four days later – Tuesday 10 July

As the plane touched down in Edinburgh Airport, Jamie felt his stomach contract to the size of a golf ball.

The team – his team – were coming home without the trophy. Scotland had been beaten by England in the third place play-off. Jamie, sitting injured in the stands, had seen the look of pure desolation on the faces of the Tartan Army. He'd felt responsible and yet entirely helpless at the same time. They'd had everything they needed to win that tournament and yet, here they were, returning home empty-handed. All they were bringing back with them were regrets.

Jamie thought back to what the dressing room had

been like after the Argentina game.

It had felt like the quietest, saddest place on earth. All of the players, even Sir Brian Robertson, had been reduced to zombies, frozen in their sorrow, paralysed in their anger and stunned in their disbelief.

They had sat and simply stared into space, the nauseating noise of the Argentinian celebrations in the dressing room next door torturing their every thought.

Then, quietly and proudly, Sir Brian Robertson had gone around the dressing room and shaken each one of his players by the hand.

Looking at the scene, Jamie had been overcome by guilt. He knew it was all his fault. If he'd told his manager the truth about his injury before it was too late, then Robertson could have replaced him with a properly fit player and they could have stopped Bertorelli and gone on and won the game. But no, Jamie's pride had got in the way. He had tried to be the hero and, instead, he'd taken the whole team down with him. Soon everyone would find out and know what he'd done – how selfish he'd been.

Robertson had come to shake Jamie by the hand as he was leaving for the hospital. All Jamie could say through his tears was: "I should have told you. I should have told you!"

*

As the aeroplane door opened, Jamie watched his teammates queue up to get off. All the players were dressed in suits to look as smart as possible for the homecoming, just in case anyone was there to greet them. Somehow, that only seemed to make it sadder.

Jamie let all the other players get off the plane first. If the fans were going to boo him, there was no need for his teammates to be subjected to that too. So he waited until the plane was almost empty. Then, slowly, Jamie picked up his crutches and hauled himself up off his seat.

He looked down at his swollen, bruised, punctured knee and wondered how long it would keep going for. Yes, he'd be able to come back from this latest injury. The scans showed that he'd probably be back playing for Hawkstone in a month. But how much damage had all those injections done? How long would his knee be able to hold out for before it gave up on him? Again.

Somewhere deep down, Jamie felt the cold chill of knowledge freeze around him. He might not have much longer left in his career.

Jamie heard cheers for his teammates and breathed a little sigh of relief. He was happy; they deserved it. They should have been coming back with the World Cup in their hands. They *had* been good enough. For a second, he allowed his mind to imagine he and his teammates walking off the plane with the famous trophy in their hands…

Finally, a minute after everyone else had got off, Jamie hauled his way to the open door.

The reaction was instant as soon as Jamie appeared. There was an explosion of noise and camera flashes. The cheers were louder than for any goal he had ever scored.

He looked up, astonished. He was speechless. There were at least twenty-thousand people there. And they were all singing his name.

One Jamie Johnson, there's only
one Jamie Johhhhnson,
There's only one Jamie Johnsooon.

Almost every single person had a banner.

But there was one banner which stood out above all the others.

Thanks for the
TARTAN PRIDE JJ

Jamie stared at it and instantly knew who'd brought it. He closed his eyes and felt a rush of such emotion that it almost overpowered him. Then he opened them and gave his mum a massive smile and wave. Sometimes, just sometimes, she knew exactly what to say.

Never in all his life had Jamie felt such warmth and appreciation from so many people. He raised one of his crutches into the air to salute the fans and then, slow and hesitant at first, he began to descend the stairs in front of the plane.

With each step, the noise seemed to get louder and louder. Jamie could feel the hairs on the back of his neck start to stand on end.

And there waiting for him at the bottom of the steps, with a camera crew in tow, was Jack Marshall.

"This is all just amazing," said Jamie, shaking his head in disbelief. "But I don't understand it. We could have done it – we were good enough, but we lost. And … I'm sorry."

"But this was a historic tournament for the country," said Jack, putting on her best TV voice. "And not only were you the inspiration for this incredible team, but, if we're to believe what we read in the newspapers, you were prepared to sacrifice a potential move to Barcelona just so you could play on for your country."

"Oh," said Jamie. "I didn't realize people knew about that."

"Well, they do," said Jack. "That was a big call to make."

"Not really," said Jamie. "Yeah, it would have been great to play for Barcelona. A proper dream and all that. But it's gone now and I don't regret it at all. Because who knows how long my career's going to last? This might be the only World Cup I ever get to play in, so I wanted to play in every minute that I could – no matter what the risks were. I wanted to do it for my teammates and for my country and that was all that I cared about. I'll never regret what I did."

The fans roared their approval.

"And *that's* why everyone is mad about Jamie Johnson," said Jack.

Jamie and Jack looked at each other and, just for a small moment in time, it was as though the cameras and the crowds weren't there…

"I'm just getting some breaking news from the tournament," said Jack suddenly, putting her hand next to her ear to hear the information that was being fed through to her.

"Jamie!" she exclaimed, looking really excited. She was sounding more and more like the old Jack, Jamie's Jack, rather than the television reporter Jack.

"Congratulations!" she said. "You've just been voted Player of the Tournament!"

"Oh, right," said Jamie, not quite sure how to react. "That's … cool."

"Cool?" laughed Jack. "It's a bit more than that! Your whole life is going to change now, Jamie. You are a … phenomenon."

This time it was Jamie's turn to blush.

"Nah," said the young superstar, shaking his head and thinking right back to where his journey had begun – all those afternoons spent kicking a ball around the park with his best mate. "Nothing's changed." He smiled. "I'm still the same guy I always was. Just a kid who loves playing football."

Final Group A Table

Team	P	W	D	L	F	A	GD	Pts
Portugal	3	2	1	0	4	1	3	7
Chile	3	1	1	1	3	2	1	4
South Africa	3	1	1	1	4	5	-1	4
Morocco	3	0	1	2	1	4	-3	1

Group A Results

Date	Fixture		
11th Jun	Sth Africa 1	- 1	Chile
11th Jun	Portugal 0	- 0	Morocco
16th Jun	Sth Africa 1	- 3	Portugal
17th Jun	Morocco 1	- 2	Chile
22nd Jun	Chile 0	- 1	Portugal
22nd Jun	Morocco 1	- 2	Sth Africa

Final Group B Table

Team	P	W	D	L	F	A	GD	Pts
Germany	3	3	0	0	7	1	6	9
Sth Korea	3	1	1	1	5	6	-1	4
Greece	3	1	0	2	2	5	-3	3
Australia	3	0	1	2	3	5	-2	1

Group B Results

Date	Fixture		
11th Jun	Sth Korea 2	- 0	Greece
12th Jun	Germany 1	- 0	Australia
16th Jun	Germany 4	- 1	Sth Korea
17th Jun	Greece 2	- 1	Australia
22nd Jun	Australia 2	- 2	Sth Korea
22nd Jun	Greece 0	- 2	Germany

Final Group C Table

Team	P	W	D	L	F	A	GD	Pts
Brazil	3	1	2	0	4	3	1	7
Russia	3	1	2	0	2	1	1	4
USA	3	1	1	1	3	3	0	4
Iraq	3	0	1	2	0	2	-2	1

	Date	Fixture
Group C Results	12th Jun	Russia 1 - 1 Brazil
	13th Jun	Iraq 0 - 1 USA
	18th Jun	USA 2 - 2 Brazil
	18th Jun	Russia 0 - 0 Iraq
	23rd Jun	USA 0 - 1 Russia
	23rd Jun	Brazil 1 - 0 Iraq

Final Group D Table

Team	P	W	D	L	F	A	GD	Pts
Argentina	3	2	1	0	6	2	4	7
Scotland	3	1	1	1	5	4	1	4
France	3	1	0	2	8	7	1	3
Nigeria	3	1	0	2	2	8	-6	3

	Date	Fixture
Group D Results	13th Jun	Scotland 0 - 1 Nigeria
	13th Jun	Argentina 2 - 1 France
	18th Jun	France 2 - 4 Scotland
	18th Jun	Nigeria 0 - 3 Argentina
	23rd Jun	France 5 - 1 Nigeria
	23rd Jun	Scotland 1 - 1 Argentina

Final Group E Table

Team	P	W	D	L	F	A	GD	Pts
Spain	3	3	0	0	5	1	4	9
Ivory Coast	3	2	0	1	4	2	2	6
Canada	3	1	0	2	3	6	-3	3
Denmark	3	0	0	3	2	5	-3	0

Group E Results

Date	Fixture
14th Jun	Spain 2 - 0 Canada
14th Jun	Ivory Coast 1 - 0 Denmark
19th Jun	Spain 1 - 0 Ivory Coast
19th Jun	Denmark 1 - 2 Canada
24th Jun	Canada 1 - 3 Ivory Coast
24th Jun	Denmark 1 - 2 Spain

Final Group F Table

Team	P	W	D	L	F	A	GD	Pts
Turkey	3	1	2	0	3	1	2	5
England	3	1	1	1	4	5	-1	4
Belgium	3	0	3	0	2	2	0	3
Egypt	3	0	2	1	4	5	-1	2

Group F Results

Date	Fixture
14th Jun	Egypt 1 - 1 Turkey
15th Jun	Belgium 1 - 1 England
20th Jun	England 0 - 2 Turkey
20th Jun	Egypt 1 - 1 Belgium
24th Jun	England 3 - 2 Egypt
24th Jun	Turkey 0 - 0 Belgium

Final Group G Table

Team	P	W	D	L	F	A	GD	Pts
Italy	3	2	1	0	5	2	3	7
Japan	3	1	2	0	7	0	7	5
Honduras	3	1	1	1	4	3	1	4
Switzerland	3	0	0	3	1	12	−11	0

Group G Results

Date	Fixture
15th Jun	Honduras 0 − 0 Japan
15th Jun	Italy 2 − 1 Switzerland
20th Jun	Italy 3 − 1 Honduras
21st Jun	Japan 7 − 0 Switzerland
25th Jun	Switzerland 0 − 3 Honduras
25th Jun	Japan 0 − 0 Italy

Final Group H Table

Team	P	W	D	L	F	A	GD	Pts
Holland	3	2	0	1	4	2	2	6
Norway	3	2	0	1	3	2	1	6
Cameroon	3	1	1	1	1	1	0	4
Croatia	3	0	1	2	0	3	−3	1

Group H Results

Date	Fixture
16th Jun	Croatia 0 − 1 Norway
16th Jun	Holland 0 − 1 Cameroon
21st Jun	Norway 1 − 0 Cameroon
21st Jun	Holland 2 − 0 Croatia
25th Jun	Cameroon 0 − 0 Croatia
25th Jun	Norway 1 − 2 Holland

WORLD CUP WALL CHART

ROUND OF 16

Portugal 2	–	3 Sth korea
Brazil 1	–	2 Scotland
Argentina 4	–	1 Russia
Germany 1	–	0 Chile
Spain 2	–	0 Italy
England 0	–	0 Norway
Turkey 4	–	2 Ivory Coast
Holland 3	–	0 Japan

England on pens 5–4

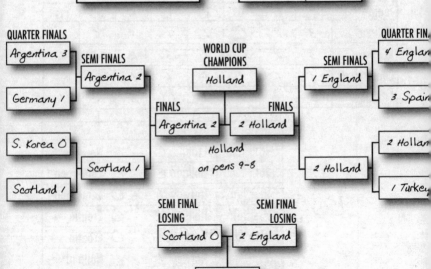

QUARTER FINALS

Argentina 3

Germany 1

S. Korea 0

Scotland 1

SEMI FINALS

Argentina 2

Scotland 1

WORLD CUP CHAMPIONS

Holland

FINALS

Argentina 2

FINALS

2 Holland

Holland on pens 9–8

SEMI FINALS

1 England

2 Holland

QUARTER FINALS

4 England

3 Spain

2 Holland

1 Turkey

SEMI FINAL LOSING

Scotland 0

SEMI FINAL LOSING

2 England

England

3rd PLACE

WORLD CUP AWARDS

Golden Boot
Shared by:
Mattheus Bertorelli (Arg) &
Dennis van der Kool (Hol)
both with 6 goals

Goal of the Tournament
Jamie Johnson
(Sco) v France

Golden Gloves Award
for Best Goalkeeper
Peter Hemschel (Nor)

Golden Whistle for
Outstanding Referee
Ricardo Barron (Ita)

Player of the Tournament –
voted by the fans
Jamie Johnson (Sco)

Coach – Sir Brian Robertson (Sco)

3-3-1-3

Hemschel
(Nor)

Clarke
(Eng)

McManus
(Sco)

Havas
(Spa)

Kurosawa
(Jap)

Richardson
(Eng)

Tarkan
(Turk)

Bertorelli
(Arg)

Bullit
(Hol)

van der Kool
(Hol)

Johnson
(Sco)

World Cup Stories

Unexpected Visitors

The day Johnson and Farrell came to my house.

Crazy Arthur Jenkins has a great story about the day Scotland World Cup heroes Jamie Johnson and Duncan Farrell turned up at his house. The problem is no one believes him!

"It was the night before the Brazil game," 70-year-old Arthur recalls. "I was just getting off to sleep when suddenly I see Johnson and Farrell on my doorstep. They were both absolutely drenched."

Although Arthur has no evidence that it was the pair of Scotland heroes and his friends have told him he must have imagined the whole thing, Arthur himself says he has no doubts.

"It was them all right," insists the grandfather of six. "I think they might have even borrowed a couple of pairs of my pyjamas. But I don't mind. I thought they were fabulous – lit up the whole tournament, and I like to think I played my part. But if they do have the time, it would be great if they could drop those pyjamas back to me. Winter's not far off now, and they were two of my best pairs."

Final ticket prices

Gwen Gobson

I won't say sorry

pledges Bertorelli

World Cup villain Mattheus Bertorelli will never say sorry for the handball which cost Scotland their World Cup dream. The Argentinian bad boy, who infamously pushed Jamie Johnson's goalbound free kick over the bar, says he would do the same thing again tomorrow.

"God tells me what to do and I obey him," claimed the forward, who was subsequently suspended from the final after his illegal intervention was caught on video. "Because of what I did, we won the game, so for me it was as good as scoring a goal."

And the feud which saw him fail to shake hands with Hawkstone club teammate Jamie Johnson before either of their World Cup clashes looks set to continue into the Premier League season too.

"I am glad I stopped him from scoring," admitted the 28-year-old, dubbed The Skilful Assassin in his homeland. "With his lies about match-fixing, he took away my freedom so I took away his goal."

I'll Be A Pro! You Can Put Your Shirt On It!

Remember the ballboy who won a legion of fans by juggling the ball in the middle of the Scotland v Argentina game before delivering it directly into Mattheus Bertorelli's unmentionables? Well, that may not be the last you see of him on the football pitch.

Cheeky Robbie Simmonds, who was lucky enough to be given Jamie Johnson's precious number 11 shirt from the titanic semi-final match against Argentina, says he's got a taste for the big time and has promised to make it all the way to the top of the football ladder.

"Loads of people have started recognizing me in the street now," laughs the 11-year-old, who became a YouTube sensation when he taunted Mattheus Bertorelli with his outrageous skills on the touchline.

"They all want to know if I'm going to be a professional. I tell them of course I am! I know Jamie Johnson because he lives near me and I've already told him I'm going to be a better player than him when I'm older! Maybe I'll even take his place in the Hawkstone team … if he can get me a trial there!"

And what of that famous Jamie Johnson number 11 shirt from the classic semi-final that is already being called one of the greatest World Cup games of all time?

"I've got it framed and above my bed," says Simmonds. "People have already offered me loads of money for it, but they're wasting their time. I wouldn't sell it for anything"

Football

Robertson: I'm Staying On

Sir Brian Robertson has agreed to stay on as Scotland manager "for the foreseeable future". The legendary coach, who says the World Cup was the best experience of his football career, has agreed to continue leading the national team whilst also carrying on his duties as Foxborough manager.

"Once I had the taste for international football, it was difficult to give it up," explained the 61-year-old, who guided Scotland to their best ever World Cup finish. "I discussed the situation with Foxborough, who have been kind enough to let me take on both jobs, as they are aware of how much my country means to me."

Robertson's inspirational leadership lit up the tournament, and although he would not be drawn on the rumours that he beat his dressing room ban by hiding in a laundry basket, he was more forthcoming on the subject of his country's star player, Jamie Johnson.

So would Robertson, in his role as Foxborough manager, be launching a transfer bid to reunite himself with outrageously talented Johnson, with whom he is said to have developed a close bond during the tournament?

"Hawkstone will want a king's ransom for Johnson", says Robertson. "I think Foxborough would have to sell Lair Park, and even then we'd still only be able to afford one of Johnson's legs!

"But I'll certainly stay in touch with Jamie. He's a great kid and he gives you absolutely everything, which is why the fans love him so much. And he's honest too. He even came up to me on the plane home to apologize for not asking to be substituted earlier in the semi-final because of his injury. He blamed himself for letting his pride get in the way. I told him that, after what he'd done for us during the tournament, he had nothing to apologize for. And, besides, real football – the best football – comes from the heart, not the head."

WAG Set to Write Autobiography

● Loretta Martin, the wannabe-WAG at the centre of a World Cup controversy with football star Jamie Johnson, has announced plans to pen her own autobiography.

Despite only being 19 years old, the former hairdresser's assistant insists she has a story worth telling.

"It's all about me," she said. "How I grew up and stuff and how everyone wants to be like me now. I get letters everyday from girls asking how they can become a WAG. I'm writing the whole book myself. I'm not using a ghost-writer or nothing. It's all me."

Martin, who is also set to launch a workout DVD and make-up range in time for Christmas, also confirmed that she is in negotiations to make a reality TV programme, with the cameras set to follow her and her family twenty-four hours a day.

"People want to know what's happening in my life," she explained. "The truth about what really happened between me and Jamie Johnson and now my new life without him. It'll be a proper wicked programme."

Red

200
plac
as r
not
con
is t

Football

Water-Way to Celebrate

The Rowing Boat goal celebration which became the trademark of Scotland's run to the World Cup semi-finals has set a new craze in schools around the country.

"All the kids are doing it," said Pete Marsden, head teacher of a high school in Caerphilly, Wales. "They love it because it's a celebration that the whole team can do together."

The celebration, in which players sit on the ground and row on an imaginary boat, was first used in Scotland's memorable victory over Brazil, although its originators, Jamie Johnson and Duncan Farrell, have never revealed the exact inspiration behind the move.

"I don't know how they got the idea but they should have trademarked it!" reckons Marsden. "It's got to be the most popular celebration out there right now!"

We invented a great goal celebration. Canoe?

Epilogue

Keep The Tartan Pride

Jamie looked at the gleaming ring and its inscription. He had honestly thought that he'd never see it again.

"So, go on, you've got to tell me everything!" he grinned. "How did you even know I'd lost it? And where was it? I looked everywhere for this," he said. Jamie slid the ring back onto his finger and breathed a huge sigh of relief. "Where was it and how did you get it back?"

"Did you look on that girl's hand?" said Jack.

"Which girl? Who do you— What? Not Loretta?"

Jack nodded. "She was in our studios doing an interview and she walked past me, bold as brass, and she was actually wearing it. I recognized it straightaway and I asked her where she'd got it from. She told me that you'd given it to her. And she kept a straight face! So it was pretty clear to me that every word that had come out of her mouth was a complete lie. You'd never give that ring to anyone, JJ. I know how important it is to you."

"See," said Jamie. "I told you… Wow! She's actually even worse than I thought. She must have nicked it the night I met her. I must have been spinning it. That little… So … but anyway … how did you get it off her? Did she just give it back to you?"

"I did what I had to do," replied Jack, more than a little mischievously. "That's all you need to know."

"Oh – you didn't, did you?" asked Jamie laughing now. "Tell me you didn't?!"

Jack flashed him her special smile.

"You did! You did your tae kwon do on her! I can't believe it! Oh, I wish I'd been there to see it!"

"Like I said: I did what I had to."

"Oh, that's brilliant!" said Jamie. "Thank you so much, Jack! Wait – so once you had the ring and realized that she'd made the whole thing up – that's when you started calling me, right?"

"Yup, but you kept ignoring my calls!"

"I did not," Jamie lied. "I was just busy!"

"Yeah, right. You put me on silent and you know it!"

Jamie smiled. What a piece of work Lorretta Martin was – she was the fakest person he'd ever met! But, on the other hand, if she hadn't have taken the ring, then Jack might never have realized that she'd been lying about everything all along and she and Jamie wouldn't be about to go on holiday together.

Jamie couldn't think of anything better. Just him and Jack – finally they were going to get to spend some time with each other. He was already off the crutches so he would be free to make the absolute most of the trip. They were going to have some serious fun.

Jamie felt his phone vibrating in his pocket. It was a strange time to ring. All Jamie's mates knew where he was going. But when he saw who it was, he had to take the call…

"Archie," said Jamie. "How you doing? Listen, I'm just in a taxi on my way to the airport. I'm with Jack and we're going to Ameri— What? Now? Why? … Oh … right … OK… But what about the injury? I probably won't even be able to train for another couple of weeks. Yeah, no I understand… OK, thanks, Archie… Yup, I'll see you there in a couple of hours."

Jamie put down the phone and stared at Jack. His eyes were glazed, trying to comprehend what he'd just been told.

"What? What is it? What's happened?" she asked.

"What's wrong, JJ?"

"No… Nothing's wrong," said Jamie. He couldn't move any of the muscles in his face. He was in a complete state of shock. The words could barely come out of his mouth.

"It's not bad news, but … we have to turn the car around."

"But we take off in four hours! What about the holiday?"

"Sorry, Jack, but we have to go back now. Straightaway," said Jamie, nervously rubbing his ring. The excitement was rapidly building and he was giving himself goosepimples as he contemplated the magnitude of what was happening.

"It's Barcelona," he said, finally, loving the sound of that magical name coming out of his mouth. "They still want to sign me, Jack! They're flying in to start talks. They arrive tonight!"

Jamie - 3 - with his granddad Mike.
(Dad says he'll play in a World
cup one day!)

Interview with Dan Freedman

You've been to the World Cup twice, what was it like?

Before becoming an author, I worked as a journalist with the England Football Team. That meant living in the team hotel, having breakfast with players like Wayne Rooney and Steven Gerrard and then going to watch them train and play in the World Cup Finals. They were some of the greatest experiences of my life. I realize how lucky I was and I thought about those times a lot when I was writing this book.

Can you do the Rainbow Flick?

Of course I can – I'm a phenomenal footballer, one of the best in the world. See, that's the good thing about being an author: you can just make stuff up.

Who are your favourite footballers at the moment?

You can't ignore Messi's majestic talent and I absolutely love the way that Xavi never ever loses the ball. Gerrard for his passion and loyalty to his club and, for the future, Jack Wilshire. So young but soooo good!

You visit lots of schools – what's the funniest question you've been asked?

Lots of kids seem fascinated to know what car I drive (a Golf, if you must know). Some ask me if I ever get bored of football (no). And one boy asked me which footballer had the biggest appetite when it came to meal times! The school visits are great fun because they are a chance for me to meet the people that I write the books for.

Who is the most famous person you've interviewed?

Take your pick: David Beckham, Cristiano Ronaldo, Sir Alex Ferguson. At the time, I had to pretend that it was no big deal and that I was all cool about it but inside I was thinking: "Oh my God! I can't believe I'm interviewing him!"

So have you ever had a kick around with Wayne Rooney?

No – I think I would be too worried about injuring him if I timed a tackle wrong! That would be a disaster! I did once get to play against Demetrio Albertini though. He was one of the best midfielders in the world when I was growing up – he won the Champions League with AC Milan. I played against him in midfield in a friendly game. Would you believe me if I told you we won?!

What inspires you to write these books?

When I was younger I wasn't a massive reader. People used to tell me to read all the time but there were no books out there that excited me. They all seemed boring. The Jamie Johnson series is for people out there who are like I was. I try to write the kind of books that I would have been desperate to read.

What's the best game you've ever been to?

In 2002, I was in Japan for the World Cup quarter-final: Brazil v England. It doesn't get much bigger than that!

Jamie Johnson books are often about triumphing over the odds. Can you give us any tips on how to become a professional footballer?

I think it's about your physical and mental dedication. Are you training as hard as you can? Are you working on your weaker foot? Do you believe in yourself? Are you trying to improve every time you play? And, if you get knocked back, how will you react? If you come back stronger, you've got half a chance.

And the other thing to remember is that even if you don't make it as a professional footballer, there are so many other jobs that you can get which involve football. Doctor, physiotherapist, coach, architect… The possibilities are all there, it's a case of going for your goals.

Want more thrilling footballing action? Catch up on Jamie Johnson's journey to the top.

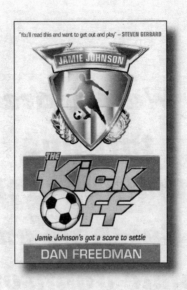

Jamie Johnson's desperate to become his school's star football player (and in his dreams, a top professional too). He's got so much to prove, and not just on the pitch – so why aren't his mum, teachers and best mate on his side?

"An inspiring read for all football fans" – GARY LINEKER

JAMIE JOHNSON

Shoot TO Win

Jamie Johnson's in it to win it

DAN FREEDMAN

Jamie Johnson can't believe his luck. He's playing for Kingfield School in a Cup semi-final and scouts from his favourite club, Hawkstone United, are coming to watch!

But Jamie's hopes of a professional career still have a long way to go…

"Jamie Johnson could go all the way" – JERMAIN DEFOE

JAMIE JOHNSON

Golden Goal

It's Jamie Johnson's time to shine

DAN FREEDMAN

There's a huge buzz around Jamie Johnson. He's being talked about as one of the country's most talented young players. But just when he's set for stardom, a shocking event threatens to end his career for ever.

Can Jamie cope with his toughest challenge yet?

"If you like football, this book's for you" – FRANK LAMPARD

Man of Match

It's crunch time for Jamie Johnson

DAN FREEDMAN

Jamie Johnson is playing the best football of his life for his beloved Hawkstone. But surviving at the top of the league isn't easy. After Hawkstone splash out on a big new signing, Jamie suddenly has a serious rival on the team. And when a series of dramatic events threaten his game, Jamie fears it could all be over…

This was the team of teams. The club of clubs. And now they wanted him to join them. A transfer to the best club in the world beckons for Jamie Johnson. This is big. This is huge!

However, a time bomb is already ticking within Jamie. . . Is the final whistle about to blow?